KU-646-934

CONTENTS

Introduction

Exploited Children is the ninety-ninth volume in the **Issues** series. The aim of this series is to offer up-to-date information about important issues in our world.

Exploited Children looks at child labour, child sexual exploitation and child soldiers.

The information comes from a wide variety of sources and includes:
Government reports and statistics
Newspaper reports and features
Magazine articles and surveys
Website material
Literature from lobby groups
and charitable organisations.

It is hoped that, as you read about the many aspects of the issues explored in this book, you will critically evaluate the information presented. It is important that you decide whether you are being presented with facts or opinions. Does the writer give a biased or an unbiased report? If an opinion is being expressed, do you agree with the writer?

Exploited Children offers a useful starting-point for those who need convenient access to information about the many issues involved. However, it is only a starting-point. At the back of the book is a list of organisations which you may want to contact for further information.

*****

Facts on child labour

International Labour Organization

One out of six children in the world today is involved in child labour, doing work that is damaging to his or her mental, physical and emotional development.

These children work in a variety of industries, and in many parts of the world. The vast majority are in the agricultural sector, where they may be exposed to dangerous chemicals and equipment. Others are street children, peddling or running errands to earn a living. Some are domestic workers, prostitutes, or factory workers. All are children who have no fair chance of a real childhood, an education, or a better life.

Children work because their survival and that of their families depend on it. Child labour persists even where it has been declared illegal, and is frequently surrounded by a wall of silence, indifference, and apathy.

But that wall is beginning to crumble. While the total elimination of child labour is a long-term goal in many countries, certain forms of child labour must be confronted immediately. An ILO study has shown for the first time that the economic benefits of eliminating child labour will be nearly seven times greater than the costs. This does not include the incalculable social and human benefits of eliminating the practice: nearly three-quarters of working children are engaged in what the world recognises as the worst forms of child labour, including trafficking, armed conflict, slavery, sexual exploitation and hazardous work. The effective abolition of child labour is one of the most urgent challenges of our time.

Key statistics

- 246 million children are child labourers.
- 73 million working children are less than 10 years old.
- No country is immune: There are 2.5 million working children in the developed economies, and another 2.5 million in transition economies.
- Every year, 22,000 children die in work-related accidents.

73 million working children are less than 10 years old

- The largest number of working children – 127 million – age 14 and under are in the Asia-Pacific region.
- Sub-Saharan Africa has the largest proportion of working children: nearly one-third of children age 14 and under (48 million children).
- Most children work in the informal sector, without legal or regulatory protection:
- 70% in agriculture, commercial hunting and fishing or forestry;
- 8% in manufacturing;
- 8% in wholesale and retail trade, restaurants and hotels;
- 7% in community, social and personal service, such as domestic work.
- 8.4 million children are trapped in slavery, trafficking, debt bondage, prostitution, pornography and other illicit activities.
- 1.2 million of these children have been trafficked.

■ The above information is from the International Labour Organization's website which can be found at www.ilo.org

© International Labour Organization

Faces of exploitation

Child labour

Many children work. After school hours children can help with household chores, fetch water, run errands, or look after their younger brothers and sisters. In this way they can participate in family life and contribute to the family income. In doing so they pick up useful skills, learn more about their own communities and prepare themselves for the responsibilities of adult life. 'Child labour', however, implies something different – that children are doing things that are harmful to their healthy development. They may be labouring long hours, sacrificing time and energy that they might have spent at school or at home, enjoying the free and formative experience of childhood.

The impact on a child

Crucially, children working for long hours are missing out on the vital opportunity that education provides to equip themselves with the knowledge, life skills and confidence to participate fully in the economic and social development of their communities and to improve their own lives. In the worst cases, they may be doing work that is physically, emotionally and/or psychologically dangerous, putting their young bodies and minds under terrible strain that can lead to permanent damage.

Most people would agree that some types of child work are evidently wrong – working in coal mines, or rubbish tips, or glass factories. But other cases are less clear cut. Much will depend on the age of the child: clearly there are some tasks that a child of sixteen might reasonably do that would be far more harmful for a child of six or eight.

The extent of the problem

How many child labourers are there? There will never be a definitive answer to this question, given inconsistencies in national standards and definitions as well as weaknesses

United Nations Children's Fund

in data collection. The most comprehensive global statistics on child labour come from the ILO (International Labour Organization), which estimated that in 2002, the number of children worldwide who were 'economically active' – doing some type of work – amounted to 352 million. Of these, 211 million were aged 5-14. But whether this activity constitutes 'child labour' depends both on the nature of the work and the age of the child. Of the 352 million economically active children, the ILO counted 246 million as 'child labourers'.

Thus some 16% of the world's children are caught up in child labour and around one in twelve children are engaged either in hazardous work or in the very worst forms of child labour. Boys and girls appear to be working to a similar extent. Girls make up around half of all child labourers, though they make up a slightly smaller proportion – around 45% – of those engaged in hazardous work.

Where are the child workers and what do they do?

Child labourers are certainly not confined to poor countries. In the industrial countries, around 2.5 million children aged 5-14 are economically active, or around 2% of the total child population. In countries with transition economies,

including former socialist countries, 2.4 million children aged 5-14, or around 4% of the total child population, are economically active. Nevertheless, the largest numbers of working children are to be found in the developing world. The most serious problems are in sub-Saharan Africa where 29% of children aged 5-14 are working (48 million), followed by Asia and the Pacific (19% or 127.3 million), Latin America and the Caribbean (16% or 17.4 million), and the Middle East and North Africa (15% or 13.4 million).

These children take on a huge variety of tasks. The majority work in agriculture, which employs 70% of child workers. This is followed by 8% working in manufacturing, and a further 8% in wholesale and retail trade, restaurants, hotels, and in various services. Most of the latter activities are performed in urban centres.

Why children work

Children work primarily because the environment they live in has failed to protect them from exploitation. A large number of factors interact to influence whether or not children will be working. These include:

- Persistent poverty – in overall terms, the dominant issue is poverty. In countries with an annual per capita income of $500 or less, the proportion of children who are working is usually between 30% and 60%, while for countries with incomes between $500 and $1,000, the proportion drops to between 10% and 30%.
- Economic shocks – a sudden family disaster, particularly death or illness, may force children to leave school and work. HIV/AIDS has now become a major factor, especially in Africa where over 28 million people are living with the disease. HIV/AIDS generally kills the main wage earners and shifts more of the

income-earning burden to children.

- Inadequate education – there is a close link between education and child labour. Education – particularly free and compulsory education of good quality up to the minimum age for entering into employment – is a key tool in preventing child labour. Attendance at school removes children, in part at least, from the labour market. As well as laying the basis for the acquisition of employable skills needed for gainful employment, school is also a place where children can be made aware of some of the risks inherent in their interaction with unscrupulous adults. The skills acquired at school may lead directly to the sort of gainful employment that will help children rise above the poverty into which they were born – and

---

Children work primarily because the environment they live in has failed to protect them from exploitation

---

thus make them, and their own children in turn, less exposed to exploitation. Furthermore, when children who have had the benefits of an education – particularly girls – grow up, they are more likely to make the choice of education for their own children, thus helping to reduce the future ranks of child labourers. Educated girls also marry later, have fewer unwanted pregnancies, and their children have lower infant mortality rates because of better health practices – all of which will contribute to

breaking the cycle of poverty that underpins the ready supply of child labourers.

- The demand for child labour – children may be pushed into work by poverty or the lack of alternatives but they can also be pulled towards work. Employers are often keen to recruit children since they will work more cheaply than adults and are likely to be more submissive. If the 'employers' are the parents, then the children's labour is free. In addition, employers may consider that some tasks are particularly suitable for children – running errands for example.

- The above information is from UNICEF UK's End Child Exploitation Campaign's website which can be found at www.endchildexploitation.org.uk

Child labour

Information from Anti-Slavery International

What is child labour?

Some types of work make useful, positive contributions to a child's development. Work can help children learn about responsibility and develop particular skills that will benefit them and the rest of society. Often, work is a vital source of income that helps to sustain children and their families.

However, across the world, millions of children do extremely hazardous work in harmful conditions, putting their health, education, personal and social development, and even their lives at risk. These are some of the circumstances they face:

- Full-time work at a very early age
- Dangerous workplaces
- Excessive working hours
- Subjection to psychological, verbal, physical and sexual abuse
- Obliged to work by circumstances or individuals
- Limited or no pay

anti-slavery
today's fight for tomorrow's freedom

'Child labour has serious consequences that stay with the individual and with society for far longer than the years of childhood. Young workers not only face dangerous working conditions. They face long-term physical, intellectual and emotional stress. They face an adulthood of unemployment and illiteracy.'
United Nations Secretary-General Kofi Annan

'We have no time for study and education, no time to play and rest, we are exposed to unsafe working conditions and we are not protected.'
Children's Forum Against the Most Intolerable Forms of Child Labour, Bangkok, 1997

- Work and life on the streets in bad conditions
- Inability to escape from the poverty cycle – no access to education

Trafficking

Trafficking involves transporting people away from the communities in which they live, by the threat or use of violence, deception, or coercion so they can be exploited as forced or enslaved workers for sex or labour. When children are trafficked, no violence, deception or coercion needs to be involved, it is merely the act of transporting them into exploitative work which constitutes trafficking.

Increasingly, children are also bought and sold within and across national borders. They are trafficked for sexual exploitation, for begging, and for work on construction sites, plantations and into domestic work. The vulnerability of these children is even greater when they arrive in another country. Often they do not have contact with their families and are at the mercy of their employers.

Why do children work?
- Most children work because their families are poor and their labour is necessary for their survival. Discrimination on grounds including gender, race or religion also plays its part in why some children work.
- Children are often employed and exploited because, compared to adults, they are more vulnerable, cheaper to hire and are less likely to demand higher wages or better working conditions. Some employers falsely argue that children are particularly suited to certain types of work because of their small size and 'nimble fingers'.
- For many children, school is not an option. Education can be expensive and some parents feel that what their children will learn is irrelevant to the realities of their everyday lives and futures. In many cases, school is also physically inaccessible or lessons are not taught in the child's mother tongue, or both.
- As well as being a result of poverty, child labour also per-petuates poverty. Many working children do not have the opportunity to go to school and often grow up to be unskilled adults trapped in poorly paid jobs, and in turn will look to their own children to supplement the family's income.

Where do children work?
- On the land
- In households – as domestic workers
- In factories – making products such as matches, fireworks and glassware
- On the street – as beggars
- Outdoor industry: brick kilns, mines, construction
- In bars, restaurants and tourist establishments
- In sexual exploitation
- As soldiers

Export industries account for only an estimated five per cent of child labour.

The majority of working children are in agriculture – an estimated 70 per cent. Child domestic work in the houses of others is thought to be the single largest employer of girls worldwide.

Case studies
Sylvia* in Tanzania worked as a domestic. Despite only being a young teenager, she worked long hours cooking, cleaning and doing the majority of household chores. She was made to sleep on the floor, was only given leftovers to eat and was not paid for her labour. When one of the men in the household severely beat her for refusing his sexual advances, she fled. A neighbour referred her to the local organisation Kivulini which provided her with safe shelter and compensation from her 'employer'.

When Ahmed* was five years old he was trafficked from Bangladesh to the United Arab Emirates to be a camel jockey. He was forced to train and race camels in Dubai for three years.

'I was scared . . . If I made a mistake I was beaten with a stick. When I said I wanted to go home I was told I never would. I didn't enjoy camel racing, I was really afraid. I fell off many times. When I won prizes several times, such as money and a car, the camel owner took every-thing. I never got anything, no money, nothing; my family also got nothing.'

Ahmed was only returned home after a Bangladesh official identified him during a visit to Dubai in November 2002. Our local partner Bangladesh National Women Lawyers' Association provided him with the specialist support and help he needed to resume his life with his family.

*Names changed

What do children want?
Children in several countries have formed their own organisations and movements to force leaders to hear their concerns and take action to improve a dire situation. Such movements include Niños y Adolescentes Trabajadores (NATS) in Latin America, the African Movement for Working Children and Youth in Africa and Bhima Sangha in South Asia.

The African Movement wants the realisation of 12 rights in particular, and they are:
- Right to vocational training
- Right to remain in our villages (not to have to go to the cities)
- Right to exercise our working activities in safety
- Right to light and limited work
- Right to rest during illness
- Right to be respected
- Right to be listened to
- Right to healthcare
- Right to learn to read and write
- Right to play and have free time
- Right to express and organise ourselves
- Right to equitable justice in case of problems.

At their fifth international conference in 2000, the Movement declared that:

'In those places where we are organised, our 12 rights have considerably progressed for us and for other working children and youth. We can now learn to read and write, we benefit from better healthcare, we can express our-selves, we are respected by every-one as well as by the judicial system, we are well treated and can work in safer environments working in a manner compatible with our capacities and can sometimes rest. We are now able to have more leisure time and fewer children leave the villages after we went to tell them of the dangers.'

- The above information is from Anti-Slavery International's website: www.antislavery.org

Child labour on sugar plantations

Foreign firms use end-product of children's hazardous work

Businesses purchasing sugar from El Salvador, including The Coca-Cola Company, are using the product of child labour that is both hazardous and widespread, Human Rights Watch said in a report released 10 June, 2004.

Harvesting cane requires children to use machetes and other sharp knives to cut sugarcane and strip the leaves off the stalks, work they perform for up to nine hours each day in the hot sun. Nearly every child interviewed by Human Rights Watch for its 139-page report, *Turning a Blind Eye: Hazardous Child Labour in El Salvador's Sugarcane Cultivation*, said that he or she had suffered machete gashes on the hands or legs while cutting cane. These risks led one former labour inspector to characterise sugarcane as the most dangerous of all forms of agricultural work.

'Child labour is rampant on El Salvador's sugarcane plantations,' said Michael Bochenek, counsel to the Children's Rights Division of Human Rights Watch. 'Companies that buy or use Salvadoran sugar should realise that fact and take responsibility for doing something about it.'

Up to one-third of the workers on El Salvador's sugarcane plantations are children under the age of 18, many of whom began to work in the fields between the ages of eight and 13. The International Labour Organization estimates that at least 5,000 and as many as 30,000 children under age 18 work on Salvadoran sugar plantations. El Salvador sets a minimum working age of 18 for dangerous occupations and 14 for most other forms of work.

Medical care is often not available on the plantations, and children must frequently pay for the cost of their medical treatment. They

> 'Child labour is rampant on El Salvador's sugarcane plantations. Companies that buy or use Salvadoran sugar should realise that fact and take responsibility for doing something about it.'
>
> Michael Bochenek, counsel to the Children's Rights Division of Human Rights Watch

are not reimbursed by their employers despite a provision in the Salvadoran labour code that makes employers responsible for medical expenses resulting from on-the-job injuries.

El Salvador's sugar mills and the businesses that purchase or use Salvadoran sugar know or should know that the sugar is in part the product of child labour. For example, Coca-Cola Co. uses Salvadoran sugar in its bottled beverages for domestic consumption in El Salvador. The company's local bottler purchases sugar refined at El Salvador's largest mill, Central Izalco. At least four of the plantations that supply sugarcane to Central Izalco regularly use child labour, Human Rights Watch found after interviewing workers.

When Human Rights Watch brought this information to the attention of Coca-Cola Co., the soft-drink manufacturer did not contradict these findings. Coca-Cola has a code of conduct for its suppliers, known as the 'Guiding Principles for Suppliers to The Coca-Cola Company,' but it is narrowly drawn to cover only direct suppliers, which includes sugar mills but excludes plantations. The guiding principles provide, for example, that the Coca-Cola Co.'s direct suppliers 'will not use child labour as defined by local law,' but they do not address the

responsibility of direct suppliers to ensure that their own suppliers do not use hazardous child labour.

'If Coca-Cola is serious about avoiding complicity in the use of hazardous child labour, the company should recognise that its responsibility to ensure that respect for human rights extends beyond its direct suppliers,' said Bochenek.

In addition, children who work on sugarcane plantations often miss the first several weeks or months of school. For example, a teacher in a rural community north of the capital San Salvador estimated that about 20 per cent of her class did not attend school during the harvest. Other children drop out of school altogether. Some children who want to attend school are driven into hazardous work because it is the only way their families can afford the cost of their education.

Up to one-third of the workers on El Salvador's sugarcane plantations are children under the age of 18

El Salvador is one of five countries in Latin America to participate in an International Labour Organization Time-Bound Programme, an initiative to address the worst forms of child labour. But officials in the Salvadoran Ministry of Labour told Human Rights Watch that most children who cut cane are simply their parents' 'helpers'.

Human Rights Watch urged El Salvador's sugar mills, Coca-Cola Co.

and other businesses that purchase Salvadoran sugar to incorporate international standards in their contractual relationships with suppliers and require their suppliers to do the same throughout the supply chain. They should also adopt effective monitoring systems to verify that labour conditions on their suppliers' sugarcane plantations comply with international standards.

■ The above information is from Human Rights Watch's website which can be found at www.hrw.org

The ILO and the fight against child labour

Eliminating child labour is an essential element in the ILO's goal of 'Decent Work for All'. The ILO tackles child labour not as an isolated issue but as an integral part of national efforts for economic and social development.

1919:
The first International Labour Conference adopts a Minimum Age (Industry) Convention (No. 5).

1930:
Adoption of the first Forced Labour Convention (No. 29).

1973:
Adoption of the Minimum Age Convention (No. 138).

1992:
The ILO establishes the International Programme on the Elimination of Child Labour (IPEC). Action includes: assessment studies, capacity building, legal reform, awareness raising and social mobilisation, prevention, withdrawal and rehabilitation of children from hazardous work, and the creation of alternatives for the families of child labourers.

1996:
Stockholm Declaration and Agenda for Action: The elaboration of the principle that a crime against a child in one place is a crime anywhere. The ILO codifies this into an international standard by developing a convention three years later which spells out the role of enforcement and penalties.

1998:
Adoption of the ILO Declaration on Fundamental Principles and Rights at Work: Freedom of association, abolition of forced labour, end of discrimination in the workplace, and elimination of child labour. All ILO Member States pledge to uphold and promote these principles.

1999:
Adoption of ILO Worst Forms of Child Labour Convention (No. 182). Focused world attention on the need to take immediate action to eradicate those forms of child labour that are hazardous and damaging to children's physical, mental or moral well-being. Ratified by 3 out of 4 ILO Member States.

2002:
The ILO establishes 12 June as World Day Against Child Labour. More than 80 countries are supported by the ILO in the formulation of their own programmes to combat child labour.

2004:
The first global economic study on the costs and benefits of eliminating child labour says the benefits will be an estimated US$ 5.1 trillion.

■ The above information is from the International Labour Organization's website which can be found at www.ilo.org

Children as domestic labourers

New report highlights plight of children working as domestic labourers

Millions of children – there is no fixed number – work night and day outside of their family homes, toiling as domestic child labourers – fetching water, minding infants, cleaning the house or tending the garden. Nearly all are exploited, exposed to hazardous work and subject to abuse. All, without exception, are at risk because of the very nature of child domestic labour. The World Day Against Child Labour 2004 shed new light on these children and what can be done to help them

For Chedita, today's visit to the centre of Manila, where throngs of child domestic workers gather once a week to play, is literally a 'walk in the park'. But it wasn't always so. Like the children – mostly girls from poor rural areas – who come to the park once a week on their sole day off to meet others like them, Chedita once worked as a domestic child labourer, logging long hours for low pay, fearing her masters and struggling to get by on little sleep, and worrying about a future without an education.

But times have changed. Now she has her education and is the president of a group which helps other girls like her find a brighter future. With the support of the ILO, the group provides shelter, legal advice and counselling, to help child domestic labourers escape abusive employers and jobs, and has lobbied successfully for laws which will eventually eliminate the practice

'There were many children in my family, we were poor and my father is disabled, so it is difficult for him to work,' Chedita recalls. 'So we decided that some of us have to work to support the others.'

How Chedita became a child domestic labourer is typical of the experiences of millions of children like her. In India, 20 per cent of all children working outside the family home are in child domestic labour.

Many suffer exploitation and abuse because working arrangements are largely informal and social protection non-existent. A wall of acceptance surrounds the practice, often considered a 'better' alternative for children from poor families.

According to Dr June Kane, author of the new ILO report, *Helping hands or shackled lives? : Understanding child domestic labour and responses to it*, the reality is very different. 'We have constantly to remind ourselves that these children are not just doing odd jobs around the house. They are in the workplace – even if that workplace is someone else 's home. But this workplace is hidden from

public view, from labour inspection, and exempt from the safeguards we put in place in legitimate work sites. The children are consequently at risk not only of exploitation but also of abuse and violence. And we see too many such cases to think that they are the exceptions.'

Not all child domestics end up without a future. ILO experience in Asia, Central and South America, and Africa shows that with strong social and national institutions, and income or credit options for the parents, children under the minimum working age can be successfully removed from domestic labour. The FNCCI, the employers' council of Nepal, has sponsored education for children who cannot immediately leave their jobs and attend school part-time.

'Child domestic labour is a waste of human talent and potential. With the help of constructive and sustainable solutions from the ILO technical cooperation programme, our constituents worldwide stand ready to put an end to this abuse,' says Frans Roselaers, Director of the ILO International Programme on the Elimination of Child Labour (IPEC). As one Nepalese child domestic worker told the ILO, 'When I see children playing in the park, I long to join them. I have to remind myself that I am just a servant.' We have to remind ourselves that they are just children and that life for them should be 'a walk in the park'.

■ For the full report, *Helping hands or shackled lives? : Understanding child domestic labour and responses to it*, see www.ilo.org/childlabour

■ The above information is from the International Labour Organization's website which can be found at www.ilo.org

Child domestics

The world's invisible workers

Summary

Child domestic workers are nearly invisible among child labourers. They work alone in individual households, hidden from public scrutiny, their lives controlled by their employers. Child domestics, nearly all girls, work long hours for little or no pay. Many have no opportunity to go to school, or are forced to drop out because of the demands of their job. They are subject to verbal and physical abuse, and particularly vulnerable to sexual abuse. They may be fired for small infractions, losing not only their jobs, but their place of residence as well.

The International Labor Organization (ILO) estimates that more girls work as domestics than in any other form of child labour. Yet they have received little attention, and even less protection. Government laws often exclude domestic workers from basic rights, ministries rarely monitor or investigate conditions of work in private households, and few programmes addressing child labour include child domestics.

In independent investigations in West Africa (2002), Guatemala (2000), El Salvador (2003), and Malaysia/Indonesia (2004), Human Rights Watch found that child domestics are exploited and abused on a routine basis. Despite the striking differences between these countries, the daily realities of the children are remarkably similar.

Central America

'The señor wanted to take advantage of me, he followed me around . . . he grabbed my breasts twice from behind while I was washing clothes in the pila. I yelled, and the boy came out, and the señor left. I didn't tell the señora, because I was afraid. I just quit.'

María A., Guatemala, describing an incident when she was fourteen or fifteen

In Guatemala and El Salvador tens of thousands of girls work as domestics, some as young as eight

years old. Human Rights Watch found that domestic workers often labour over fifteen hours a day, or ninety hours a week, for wages much lower than those of other workers. Like domestics in most other countries, they are routinely subject to verbal and emotional abuse from their employers, and are particularly vulnerable to sexual harassment and sexual violence from men living in or associated with the household.

According to one local advocate in Guatemala, employers control nearly every aspect of a domestic worker's life, including 'the salary she earns, the work she does, her working hours, the days she can go out, where she can go and even what language she should speak in the home and how she should dress'.

Domestic work frequently interferes with schooling. Many domestics

have no opportunity to attend school. Others drop out, most commonly because their work hours conflict with the school day or because of school fees and other education-related expenses. Some are able to attend night classes, but travelling to and from school at night involves increased risks to their safety.

Seventeen-year-old Flor N. works thirteen hours each day as a domestic worker in San Salvador, beginning at 4.30 a.m. 'It's heavy work: washing, ironing, taking care of the child,' she told Human Rights Watch. When she finishes her workday, she heads to her fifth grade evening class. 'Sometimes I come to school super tired . . . I get up at 2 a.m. to go to work.' When she rises at 2 a.m. to return to work, she must walk one kilometre along a dangerous road to catch a minibus. The only domestic worker for a household of four adults and a three-year-old, she is also responsible for preparing their lunch, dinner, and snacks, and she watches the child. 'Sometimes I eat, but sometimes I am too busy,' she told us. 'There is no rest for me. I can sit, but I have to be doing something.'

Economically active children

Estimates of economically active children (aged 5-14) in 2000[1]

Region	Number of economically active children (millions)	Percentage of global total by group	Percentage of economically active children in total child population[1]
Developed (industrialised) economies	2.5	1	2
Transition economies	2.4	1	4
Asia and the Pacific	127.3	60	19
Latin America and the Caribbean	17.4	8	16
Sub-Saharan Africa	48	23	29
Middle East and North Africa	13.4	6	15
Total	211	–	16

1 These estimates are prone to higher error rates than the corresponding global estimates as a result of the reduced number of data sets available for their calculation. Rounding errors mean that percentage totals do not equal 100. The groupings follow the categories adopted in the ILO Key Indicators of the Labour Market (KILM). The total number of children aged 5-14 in the world in 2000 was approximately 1,200 million, of which the Asia-Pacific region accounted for 28 per cent and sub-Saharan Africa for 7.4 per cent.

Sources: ILO Bureau of Statistics and United Nations Population Division

She has only one day off each month and receives wages of about US $26/month for her labour.

In Guatemala, most domestic workers migrate from rural villages to work in urban households. Many are Mayan, and are routinely subject to ethnic discrimination. A Keqchikel girl told Human Rights Watch that when she was fourteen, she worked seventeen hours a day, with only ten minutes to eat lunch and dinner. Her employers gave her 'a different class of food' than they ate themselves, and would not let her eat near them. 'They treated me poorly because I wear traje (traditional dress),' she said.

One-third of the domestic workers Human Rights Watch interviewed in Guatemala reported having suffered some kind of un-wanted sexual approaches by men living in or associated with the household. Few domestic workers feel they can tell the woman of the house about such abuse; most simply quit and look for another job.

Both the Guatemalan and Salvadoran codes effectively exclude domestics from basic rights. Unlike most other workers, they are denied the nationally-recognised eight-hour workday. Domestics commonly receive wages that are lower than the minimum wages in other sectors of employment.

Salvadoran government officials often deny that children, particularly those under the mini-mum employment age of fourteen, work in domestic service in large numbers. An ILO study on work in domestic service concluded that it was among the worst forms of child labour, but the Salvadoran govern-ment has not included domestic labour in its ILO Time-Bound Programme, an initiative to elimin-ate the worst forms of child labour within a period of five to ten years.

Indonesia/Malaysia

'I took care of two children . . . I cleaned all parts of the house, washed the floor, washed clothes, ironed, cleaned the walls, and washed the car. I cleaned two houses, because I also cleaned the grandmother's house. I worked from 4 a.m. to 7 p.m. I had no rest during the day. I worked every day

and was not allowed to go out, not even to walk on the street. The lady employer yelled at me every day. She slapped me one or two times a week. My employer kept my passport. I was scared to run away without my passport. I wanted to run away, but I was afraid the Malaysian government and security would catch me. I had to buy my own ticket home. [When I returned to Indonesia,] I called the recruitment company in Jakarta to complain about my salary, but they didn't want to take my call.'

Srihati H., seventeen years old, former Indonesian migrant domestic worker in Malaysia

Approximately 200,000 Indonesian girls and women work in Malaysia as household domestics. Human Rights Watch interviews in 2004 with Indonesian migrant workers, Indonesian government officials, and agents suggest that many girls migrate for work abroad with altered ages on their travel documents, masking the number of girls in official statistics. Suwari S. told Human Rights Watch, 'There were a lot of young girls [in the recruitment training centre], the youngest was fifteen. They changed my age to twenty-six; I was sixteen at the time.'

Child domestic workers en-counter abuses at every stage of the migration process, including recruit-ment, training, employment, and return. Indonesian girls seeking employment abroad encounter unscrupulous agents, discriminatory hiring processes, and months-long confinement in overcrowded train-ing centres. In order to pay recruit-ment and processing fees, they either take large loans requiring repayment at extremely high interest rates or the first four or five months of their salary is deducted. Recruiters often

fail to provide complete informa_ about job responsibilities, wor_ conditions, or where the girls can turn for help if they face abuse. Girls expecting to spend one month in pre-departure training facilities are often trapped in heavily guarded centres for three to six months without any income, or may be trafficked into forced labour, including forced domestic work or forced sex work.

Once employed as domestic workers in Malaysia, Indonesian girls and women typically work sixteen-hour days, seven days a week, with no overtime pay and with no scheduled rest. Domestic workers in Malaysia are not allowed outside of the house and many reported they were unable to write letters home, make phone calls, or practise their religion. Many employers withhold payment of wages until the standard two-year contract is completed, making it difficult for girls to escape from abusive situations. At the end of the contract, many do not receive their full wages, and if they do, receive US $90-100 per month, amounting to less than $0.25 per hour. Employers and agents routinely confiscate the passports of domestic workers, making it difficult for them to escape. The rigid enforcement of Malaysia's draconian immigration laws mean that workers caught without docu-ments are often indefinitely detained and deported without being able to present their complaints about abusive employers.

Abuses against child domestics are compounded by the lack of legal protection for domestic workers in Malaysia's employment laws, and the limited possibilities for redress. Malaysia's employment laws specific-ally exclude basic protections for domestic workers, including those governing hours of work, rest days, and compensation for accidents. There are no mechanisms for monitoring workplace conditions, and the resolu-tion of most abuse cases is left to private, profit-motivated agencies often guilty of committing abuses themselves. Bilateral agreements between Indonesia and Malaysia fail to provide adequate protections for domestic workers, and do not include protections for child workers.

...ndonesia have both
...nvention 182 on the
...f the Worst Forms of
...r, but enforcement
...

W... and Central Africa

'In the beginning, she [my boss] was nice to me, but then she changed. Any time I did something wrong, she would shout at me and insult me. Sometimes she would tell her friends what I had done, and they would come over and beat me . . . She would curse me and say I had no future.'

Assoupi H., sixteen, a child domestic worker in Togo

In West and Central Africa, girls as young as seven provide a cheap workforce to families needing assistance with housework or small commercial trades. They work long days performing a variety of tasks, such as selling bread, fruit or milk in the market, grilling skewers of meat on the roadside, or working in a small boutique. Some describe selling bread in the market from 6 a.m. until 7 p.m, then returning home to bake bread for the next day. Others are forced to spend all day pounding fufu, a doughy paste made of mashed yams or cassava. When not working in markets, girls perform domestic chores such as preparing meals, washing dishes, or caring for young children. One sixteen-year-old girl was trafficked to Togo when she was only three. 'I had to fetch water for the house, sweep, wash the dishes, and wash clothes,' she said. 'I would bathe the children, cook for them, and wash their clothes. When they were young, they cried a lot.'

Child domestics work under constant threat of punishment and physical abuse. 'If I lost any yam in the pounding, the woman beat me – slapped me with her hand,' a Togolese girl reported. Another said, 'If we didn't sell all the bread in one day, she [the boss] would beat us with a stick.' In interviews with Human Rights Watch, girls described being struck with blunt objects and electric wire, and threatened with punishment and sometimes death. Many escaped following an incident of unendurable abuse, after which they lived abandoned in the street. Girls also faced the risk of sexual abuse by older men or boys living in the same house or when living in the street.

Child domestic work is linked to the broader phenomenon of child trafficking, which occurs along numerous routes in West and Central Africa. The United Nations estimates that 200,000 children are recruited for exploitation each year in the region that includes Benin, Burkina Faso, Cameroon, Côte D'Ivoire, Gabon, Ghana, Mali, Nigeria, and Togo. Child traffickers capitalise on a combination of entrenched poverty and weak child protection laws, as well as a high demand for cheap labour in host countries. Children orphaned by HIV/AIDS or other causes may be dis-proportionately vulnerable due to the stigma they face, as well as the economic pressures caused by the loss of a breadwinner. Child trafficking is also linked to the denial of education, especially for girls, who may be the first to be withdrawn from school to earn a living. A number of children report that the prohibitive cost of school supplies or uniforms forces them to withdraw from school, after which they are recruited by child traffickers.

Some countries in the region have enacted anti-trafficking legislation in compliance with the UN Protocol to Prevent, Suppress and Punish the Trafficking of Persons (2000), but such laws remain poorly enforced. Gabonese authorities reportedly conduct periodic round-ups of child labourers and arrange for their repatriation to their country of origin. Employers and traffickers are rarely prosecuted, however. While some bilateral and multilateral repatriation agreements exist, efforts to negotiate a regional anti-trafficking convention stalled in 2002. Governments also fail to provide adequate protection to trafficked children. While some short-term shelters exist, follow-up and rehabilitation are rarely con-ducted, and a lack of child protection measures often allows children to be re-trafficked multiple times.

■ The above information is from Human Rights Watch's website which can be found at www.hrw.org
© *Human Rights Watch*

Conclusions

The large numbers of girls working as domestic labourers, and the extreme exploitation and abuse that they endure requires that the international community prioritise protection for child domestics as part of strategies to end child labour. Key steps that governments can take to protect the rights of child domestics include the following:

■ Establishing an unequivocal minimum age for employment and explicitly prohibiting the employment of all children under the age of eighteen in harmful or hazardous labour.

■ Amending national laws as necessary to ensure that domestic workers receive the same rights as other workers, including a minimum wage, time off, and limits on hours of work.

■ Launching public information campaigns on the rights of domestic workers and responsibilities of employers, with special emphasis on the situation of child domestic workers and the potential hazards they face.

■ Ensuring that all children enjoy the right to a free basic education by eliminating formal school fees and other obstacles to education, and by identifying and implementing strategies to reduce other costs to attending school, such as transportation, school supplies, and uniforms.

■ Creating a confidential toll-free hotline to receive reports of workers' rights violations, including abuses against child domestics.

■ Creating effective mechanisms for inspection, enforcement, and monitoring of child labour, and promptly investigating any complaints of abuses against child domestics.

■ Taking all appropriate law enforcement measures against perpetrators of physical and/or sexual violence against child domestics.

■ Ensuring care and support to children who escape domestic labour and have suffered physical or sexual violence, including treatment of sexually transmitted diseases.

Child labour – what can be done?

There is no simple answer

It's easy to get overwhelmed by the issue and then proceed to dismiss it. This cannot continue to happen. In papers prepared by UNICEF, for a 1997 International Conference on Child Labour, the authors revealed that child labour can best be combated through education; social awareness and activism; the removal and rehabilitation of child labourers; legislation and proper enforcement of those laws. Governments need to devote resources to education so that schooling is compulsory, of good quality and relevance, and is of little or no cost financially to poor families. In 1994, Malawi made primary education free. From one academic year to the next, enrolment increased by roughly 50 per cent, and more of the new students were female than male. The international community has the funds to provide free primary education. It's a question of budgeting priorities.

The following initiatives can be effective in combating child labour. This list is not exhaustive.

Improving child labour legislation and laws

Many countries have national child labour laws that establish a minimum age for work and regulate working conditions. These laws tend to be effective in combating child labour

abuses in the formal sector (the sector of the economy which lawfully employs people and pays taxes) in urban areas. However, especially in developing countries, legal protection for child labourers does not extend beyond the formal sector to the kinds of work in which children are most involved, such as agriculture and domestic service. In addition, labour laws in many countries do not cover factories employing less than ten people. The carpet industry in Pakistan, for example, is largely a cottage industry, deliberately organised in this way to avoid labour laws. It is, therefore, important to extend protection so that laws cover the main places where children work, and the most exploitative forms of child labour.

Enforcement of child labour legislation and laws

Lack of enforcement, especially in the main areas in which children work and are exploited, is the key obstacle to combating child labour. Laws cannot be effective if they are not enforced.

Increasing access, quality and relevance of education

Education is the key to ending the exploitation of children. If an education system is to attract and retain children, its quality and relevance must be improved, as well. Children who attend school are less likely to be involved in hazardous or exploitative work.

The main obstacle to achieving universal primary education is the inability and/or the unwillingness of governments to provide adequate and quality educational facilities for poor children in rural areas and in city shantytowns. Evidence from around the world has shown that poor families are willing to make sacrifices to send their children to school when it is economically and physically accessible and truly productive in terms of future employment prospects. With children in school, their unemployed adult relatives may take their places. These adults could unite to form trade unions and demand both livable wages and safe, healthy work environments.

The focus should not just be on education of children. Emphasis should also be on education programmes for adults, especially women. Evidence shows that there is an inverse relationship between adult literacy rates and the incidence

Children engaged in child labour

Numbers and percentages of children engaged in economic activity, child labour and worst forms of child labour in 2000 (by age)

	5-14 years		15-17 years		Total	
	Number (millions)	Percentage of age group	Number (millions)	Percentage of age group	Number (millions)	Percentage of age group
Economically active children	210.8	18	140.9	42	351.7	23
of which: Child labourers	186.3	16	59.2	18	245.5	16
■ of which: Children in worst forms of child labour	–	–	–	–	178.9	11.5
■ Children in hazardous work	111.3	9	59.2	18	170.5	11
■ Children in unconditional worst forms	–	–	–	–	8.4	0.5

– = figures not available.

Source: ILO estimates for 2000 and World Population Prospects: The 2000 Revision. Vol. 2 The sex and age distribution of the world population (New York, United Nations, 2001)

of child labour in the long run. Educated adults have fewer and better-educated children.

Vocational training
Vocational education and training for older child labourers can play an important role in combating child labour. Training provides the marketable skills for gainful employment, which in turn contribute to local and national development.

Equality for women and girls
The campaign to abolish child labour cannot be separated from women's struggles for recognition, decision-making power, autonomy, equality with men, a fair division of paid and unpaid work, and other measures to end poverty and violence. The social welfare of children is closely related to the position of women. Throughout the world, it is women who spend the most time caring for children. Women are the hardest hit by World Bank and IMF Structural Adjustment Programmes: their spending power is reduced; their workload is increased; and they are often left to care for families alone. They may have no choice but to let the children work for the sake of the family as a whole. As soon as a woman's income improves, so too does the situation of her children. Women invest in their children: in their food, water, housing, clothing, and schooling. Women need access to decent jobs and good childcare. A commitment to women's equality must be part of the commitment to end child labour.

Replace child workers with adults
Because so many families depend on their children's income to survive, solutions are needed that won't plunge families further into poverty. Replacing child workers with their parents (who may be unemployed) would actually increase a family's income because adults are more highly paid. The small increase in production costs which would result from replacing child workers with adults would have a small effect on sales in importing countries. Research carried out in the hand-made carpet industry shows that the cost of replacing children with adults

> *Research carried out in the hand-made carpet industry shows that the cost of replacing children with adults in factories only adds about 4% to the price of a carpet*

in factories only adds about 4% to the price of a carpet. This would not mean losing all-important export markets: surveys show importers will pay up to 15% more.

How can consumers know if what they're buying is made by child labour?
Consumers can keep their eyes open for labels stating that the product is union made, or watch for the labels of campaigns such as Rugmark and Fairtrade mark. These types of labels provide a guarantee that children were not involved in the production of the item. Also, if you don't know (which is often the case) . . . ask! The sales staff may be able to provide you with the information you need. Then contact the company explaining your concern.

Shouldn't we boycott?
Boycotts are a matter of debate, particularly with respect to their lifespan and effectiveness. There have been successes, such as the boycott campaign against the Apartheid government in South Africa. But boycotts can also fail to achieve their results, so it is important to have a clear outcome and to decide on an endpoint to prevent the boycott from dragging on. Ethical consumerism can be a powerful force in influencing consumers. A more sophisticated campaign (as opposed to boycotts) against a company, for example, would not only involve drawing public attention to the company using child labour, but also encourage the company to improve conditions for their workers.

We need to put pressure on governments and entire industries to stop child labour and to provide assistance and alternatives for child labourers. The international labour movement has recently negotiated an agreement with FIFA, the world soccer federation. FIFA promises that they will no longer put their industry seal on soccer balls made by children. Nike, Reebok, and the soccer ball manufacturers will now be forced to help pay to get kids back in schools, and will have to employ adults instead of children. ARTSANA, a multi-national toy manufacturer, has also signed an agreement that protects basic human and trade union rights as well as international labour and environmental regulations. The deal, reached with Italian trade unions, includes provisions that: establish a minimum age for workers; regulate hours of work; put an end to forced labour and guarantee a safe work environment.

FUNKY IMPORTED BRACELETS

Does Nike use child labour?

From 1996 to 1999, there was a lot of media attention on Nike and its use of child labour. An article appeared in major magazines and newspapers in the USA showing pictures of children stitching soccer balls in Pakistan. Nike came under a lot of criticism, as did all of the major multinational sports companies in south Asia that used child labour. Since then, Nike has gone to great measures to eliminate child labour from its production and 'out sourcing', as have most major corporations, because of the stigma attached. The problem, however, with Nike as with most major corporations is not that they still 'directly' use child labour, but that 'they are responsible for child labour in an indirect way'. When multinational corporations do not pay their workers in the developing world a just and livable wage, children must still work to help their families survive. Children work in other areas of child labour, selling things on the streets, or as domestics, for example. We must hold major corporations accountable for indirectly causing child labour through sweatshop labour of the family member they hire. We must strive to eliminate sweatshop labour of the adult worker in the family if we want to eliminate child labour. We must challenge companies to pay their employees a livable wage, so that children in every family can be freed from child labour and sent to school.

What needs to be done to combat child labour? (Summary)

- Reduce poverty so there is less need for children to work.
- Increase adults' wages so there is less need for children to work. Adults need a living wage.
- Improve working conditions so that children's health and safety are ensured.
- Shorten children's working hours so they can attend school.

- Ban hazardous and exploitative work such as bonded labour, sex work, military conscription, mining and all work that exposes children to toxic substances or extreme temperatures.
- Make education more attractive and relevant to children's needs.

■ The above information is from Free the Children. For further information, visit their website: www.freethechildren.com

Child labour

International instruments protecting children against harmful forms of labour

UN Convention on the Rights of the Child
Article 32
'the right of the child to be protected from economic exploitation and from performing any work that is likely to be hazardous or to interfere with the child's education or to be harmful to the child's health or physical, spiritual, moral or social development.'

ILO Convention (No. 182) on the Prohibition and Immediate Action for the Elimination of the Worst Forms of Child Labour
Article 3 the worst forms of child labour include:
a. all forms of slavery or practices similar to slavery, like trafficking of children, debt bondage, forced recruitment in armed conflict,
b. the use of a child for prostitution or pornography,
c. the use of a child for illicit activities, like the production and trafficking of drugs,
d. work which, by its nature or the circumstances in which it is carried out, is likely to harm the health, safety or morals of children.

Other relevant international conventions:
ILO Convention (No.138) on the Minimum Age for Admission to Employment
   Optional Protocols to the CRC on the involvement of children in armed conflict and on the sale of

> ### Article 3 the worst forms of child labour include all forms of slavery or practices similar to slavery

children, child prostitution and child pornography

ILO Conventions (No.29 and 105) on Forced or Compulsory Labour

1921
International Convention for the Suppression of the Traffic in Women and Children

1949
Convention for the Suppression of the Traffic in Persons and of the Exploitation of the Prostitution of Others

1956
Supplementary Convention on the Abolition of Slavery, the Slave Trade, and Institutions and Practices Similar to Slavery.

■ The above information is from ChildHope's website which can be found at www.childhopeuk.org

Economic truths of child labour

By John Blundell

Every high street in Scotland offers us items created by people whose poverty we can barely imagine. The tea in our cups was plucked by young women earning pennies in Sri Lanka. Our coffee has similar origins.

Now we are learning that fashionable trainers were crafted by children in grim circumstances in Laos or the Philippines.

The International Labour Organisation (ILO), an arm of the United Nations, has just published a report outlining these horrors and urging steps the world should take to suppress child labour. It says that one in six children are at work between their sixth and 17th birthdays. The occurrence of child labour seems a good barometer of local poverty.

The ILO's arguments are more than moral outrage – they also say the children are of less economic value without decent schooling.

I don't contest the good intentions of these arguments. I'm sure I'd be pained if I saw children in workshops in Cambodia or Somalia. Yet for the ILO's economic literacy, I give low marks: suppressing child labour would only deepen misery.

In its foggy way, the ILO argues parents should be paid the equivalent of their child's market value, replacing the income forfeited if the child attends school instead. It is ambiguous where this money would come from but presumably through taxation of the population – i.e., the parents.

It is easy for us to 'tut' about child labour from our capitalist affluence. If you live in the deeply impoverished nations where markets have been suppressed or deformed, your only asset is your ability to work, and that of your children.

Sometimes I find people assume children did nothing more than picnic and play happily until the evil capitalists forced them into textile mills and down the mines after the Industrial Revolution. The truth is that child labour was the reality of life in all rural economies long before Dickens got on the case of child chimney sweeps.

It was the rise of capitalism that permitted the extended years of leisure we call education. Working in the newly-emerging factories was regarded as a far better option than slaving in the fields – linen was more profitable than turnips.

> **The truth is that child labour was the reality of life in all rural economies long before Dickens got on the case of child chimney sweeps**

Child labour is not the modern invention of 'globalisation'. All farming has always used children. Scotland's school summer holidays exist not so everyone can fly down to the Spanish Costas, but so children are free to help with the harvest. To learn rural skills was the reality of education in most of human history. In more urban areas, the young would learn other appropriate skills.

I believe that working in scruffy factories in Manila or Nairobi is an opportunity for the people involved. Making fashion garments or chic trainers for eventual sale on Princes Street offers far greater benevolence than the humbugging of overseas aid. Aid is famously described as a device by which the poor people in the West fund the rich of the Third World. But free trade in shirts transfers money from the rich of the West to the poor of the East.

All the US democratic presidential candidates have been out-shouting each other about child labour as a malignancy caused by globalisation. Our own politicians are apprehensive about 'asylum seekers', the new euphemism for immigration. Do people try to flock westwards because of our crazy policies? Or do they look for a solution to the economic problems they have in their own country?

The biggest single preventable cause of poverty is the European Union's agricultural policies. Affluence could spread across the planet if we opened our markets to non-EU foodstuffs. I remain baffled why no Scottish politician campaigns to cut the price of our groceries.

Would it not be popular? I'm not advocating sending any child into dangerous or degrading roles, but I do believe every school could allow pupils to widen their knowledge and experience by participating in local commercial life. It could be fun. It could be life-changing. Many of Scotland's young are held captive in schools that bore them and alienate them. All that we seem willing to accept is newspaper rounds and there is even talk in Brussels of banning them. Participating in your community's shops, say, can only widen experience. We regard student jobs as a degradation. It ought to be part of growing up.

As the economies of Asia accelerate, the number of children working tumbles as parents prefer to buy education. They know an educated child should earn more and so help the extended family. Self-interest must be a better guide than abstract good intentions from the ILO's office block in Geneva.

Next time you are exploring the ever cheaper wares in your favourite shops, look at the origin labels. The people who produce these items are richer than they would be without production lines near their homes.

A pernicious argument is that children working stop adults earning full wages. This is precisely the economic dunce-speak that used to argue a woman's place is in the home. Adam Smith argued that a poor man's poverty can be his asset, he can trade or work his way up. The Third World's great advantage is their relative cheapness. Muddled, if kindly, thinking wants to suppress this.

Rich countries should welcome the new nations joining the markets. Child labour will evaporate as prosperity spreads. In the meantime, Scottish pupils might find a day's work far more educational than torture by blackboard.

■ John Blundell is director general of the Institute of Economic Affairs.

■ This article first appeared in *The Scotsman*, 23 February 2004. For more information visit the Institute of Economic Affairs' website at www.iea.org.uk

Eliminating child labour

ILO study: eliminating child labour will be costly, but will yield enormous economic benefits

Can child labour really be eliminated, and if so, how much would it cost? A new study says it can, and that the financial returns would vastly outweigh the societal investments. World of Work asked Peter Dorman, author of the study* prepared for the ILO International Programme on the Elimination of Child Labour (IPEC), how these costs and benefits were calculated.

World of Work: What are the costs and benefits of eliminating child labour?
Peter Dorman: We put the costs at around US$760 billion, while the benefits would be an estimated US $5.1 trillion in the developing and transitional economies, where most child labourers are found. This seems a huge commitment, but pales in comparison to other costs borne by developing countries. Average annual costs would amount to about 20 per cent of current military spending, or 9.5 per cent of debt service.

World of Work: The ILO estimates that some 246 million children are currently involved in child labour. What are the main costs of removing them from work?
Dorman: The cost of increasing the quantity and quality of education to accommodate all the world's children formed nearly two-thirds of total costs. This entailed building new schools, training and hiring new teachers and supplying educational materials.

World of Work: Still, child labourers provide vital income to their families. What happens when they stop working?
Dorman: There is an 'opportunity cost of eliminating child labour' – the income families lose when their children are removed from work and sent to school. So we calculated the cost of setting up income transfer programmes to compensate these families, and for intervention programmes to urgently eliminate the worst forms of child labour.

World of Work: How did you calculate the benefits?
Dorman: The two major benefits – improved education and improved health – both translate into economic gains. With universal education for children to age 14, we calculated that each child would benefit from 11 per cent more future income for every extra year of schooling. Also, by eliminating the worst forms of child labour and the toll it takes on human health and productivity, many countries would experience tangible economic gains.

World of Work: How can this be implemented?
Dorman: The study was based on an ideal, standardised programme. But in the real world, country-specific programmes, like those already set into motion by the ILO, are required to effectively eliminate child labour. The study has asked the right questions: What are the costs of taking children out of work and sending them to school? What are the long-term benefits? Now that we have these answers, there is a strong economic case behind the campaign to eliminate child labour.

Investing in every child: An economic study of the costs and benefits of eliminating child labour, ILO 2004, ISBN 92-2-115419-X. Available at www.ilo.org/publications, or can be downloaded in pdf format at www.ilo.org/ipec. For more information, see the press release at www.ilo.org/communication

■ The above information is from *World of Work*, No. 51, June 2004, published by the International Labour Organization (ILO).

Commercial sexual exploitation

Information from UNICEF

The commercial sexual exploitation of children is child sexual abuse in exchange for some sort of payment, either money or favours. Children are directly used for sex and/or used in pornography. The sexual exploitation of children is a serious crime and against the law in every country.

Children may be 'trafficked' – transported to another place, either within or outside their own country, for the purpose of exploitation, such as forced labour or prostitution. Or they may be exploited by an adult who has a continuing abusive relationship with a child, offering rewards, gifts or protection in exchange for sex.

Because the exploitation of children is often hidden, there are no reliable figures about how many children are exploited. But the number is thought to be up to two million a year (International Labour Organization). Most are girls, but a significant number are boys.

> ### Because the exploitation of children is often hidden, there are no reliable figures about how many children are exploited

This exploitation happens all over the world: in rich countries and in poor. For example, according to studies:

- there are between 40,000 and 60,000 children in prostitution in the Taiwan Province of China;
- 25 per cent of all people in prostitution in Tulear, Madagascar, are children;

- in the United States, one in five children who use the Internet regularly are approached by strangers for sex;
- in Mexico, more than 16,000 children are involved in prostitution;
- in Lithuania, 20-50 per cent of people in prostitution are children. Children as young as 11 are known to work in brothels, and some children between 10 and 12 years old living in out-of-home care have been used to make pornographic films.

Sexual exploitation happens in many different locations, including on the street, in brothels, in private homes, and in tourist facilities, such as hotels.

All commercial sexual exploitation of children involves an abuse of power: adults or other children taking advantage of their greater wealth, status and physical strength.

All sexually exploited children suffer serious physical, psychological and social harm. The exploitation may involve rape or other physical and mental violence. In addition, children have a high risk of being infected with HIV and other sexually transmitted infections, because young bodies are generally more vulnerable to damage from sex, and because children are often not able to control when and with whom they have sex, or whether a condom is used.

Children who are sexually exploited or abused are victims of a crime. No child can ever be said to have 'chosen' to be sexually exploited or is to blame for what happens to them. Children turn to prostitution when they have no other options.

The solution to the problem must involve a broad range of measures, including:

- reducing poverty and improving access to education in a safe school environment, so children have more options and are better equipped to protect themselves;

- changing attitudes, so the problem is not kept hidden because of shame, so that girls and women are never regarded as property or second-class citizens, and so that adults and children are less likely to think of children in a sexual way;
- passing and enforcing appropriate laws that punish exploiters and abusers, and not victims;
- finding ways of identifying and supporting children at risk, and helping sexually abused and exploited children return to their communities.

- The above information is from UNICEF's website which can be found at www.unicef.org

Sexual exploitation

Information from Free the Children

Protection of children from sexual exploitation

One of the most important campaigns that Free the Children is involved in is protecting children from sexual exploitation, or prostitution. Laws are being made worldwide to prevent and punish sexual offenders who commit these crimes outside their own countries, which is also known as sexual tourism. Foreigners and citizens alike should not be exempt from following the United Nations Convention on the Rights of the Child's laws concerning the safety and well-being of children.

The Declaration and Action for Agenda of the World Congress Against Commercial Sexual Exploitation of Children (1996) provides the following definition of the commercial sexual exploitation of children:

■ 'The Commercial sexual exploitation of children is a fundamental violation of children's rights. It comprises sexual abuse by the adult and remuneration in cash or in kind to the child or to a third person or persons. The child is treated as a sexual object and as a commercial object. The commercial sexual exploitation of children constitutes a form of coercion and violence against children, and amounts to forced labour and a contemporary form of slavery.'

There are three main and interrelated forms of commercial sexual exploitation of children:

■ Prostitution
■ Pornography
■ Trafficking for sexual purposes

Other forms of sexual exploitation of children include sex tourism and early marriages (the marriage of children under the age of 18). The International Labour Organization includes commercial sexual exploitation of children as one of the worst forms of child labour under Convention 182 concerning the Worst Forms of Child Labour.

The Optional Protocol on the Convention on the Rights of the Child on the Sale of Children, Child Prostitution and Child Pornography entered into force in January 2002. It can be reached at: www.unhchr.ch/html/menu2/dopchild.htm With this protocol, states agree to prohibit the sale of children, child prostitution and child pornography.

Helpful facts

■ The commercial sexual exploitation of children is estimated to be a multi-billion-dollar industry, drawing in over 1 million children each year worldwide.

■ The 'sex tourism' industry, involving men travelling to other countries to engage in sex with children, has been documented in the Philippines, Cambodia, Thailand, and countries in North America and Eastern Europe. Most of the children exploited in the sex trade are between the ages of 13 and 18, although there is evidence of children younger than 5 being sexually exploited as well.

■ The worst-affected area for child prostitution is Asia, where one million children are sexually exploited. An estimated 30,000 children in India are in the sex trade, along with between 80,000 and 800,000 children in Thailand.

■ Approximately 30% of the 185,000 prostitutes in Vietnam are thought to be under the age of 16.

■ In Latin America, approximately 25,400 children are engaged in prostitution in the Dominican Republic, and 3,000 children were sexually exploited in Colombia's capital, Bogota, alone.

■ A recent survey indicated that an estimated 5,000 children are involved in prostitution, pornography, and sex tourism in Mexico. Most of them are street children.

■ In Africa, sexual exploitation of children is on the rise over the whole continent. In South Africa, of the country's 40 million people, 70,000 women and girls are believed to be working in the sex trade.

■ In Africa, young boys are often recruited into the armed forces not only to fight, but also to sexually service the soldiers.

■ A large portion of child prostitutes catch sexually transmitted diseases (including HIV/AIDS), are forced to have abortions, and suffer serious psychological problems.

■ One study found that 60 to 70% of child prostitutes in Thailand are HIV infected.

■ Many circumstances, such as poverty, lack of education, and parental pressure force children into the sex industry. Many families, however, mistakenly send their children into what they believe to be domestic servitude. The children are then kidnapped, trafficked across borders, and forced to work as sex slaves.

How you can help

The commercial sexual exploitation of children is a grave violation of the Convention on the Rights of the Child and must be stopped. You can play a role!

- Pressure your government to develop and enforce laws, policies and programmes to combat commercial sexual exploitation of children.

  Free the Children's advocacy campaign in the area of commercial sexual exploitation of children has been very successful. Free the Children was instrumental in helping to pressure the governments of Canada, Mexico and Italy to make changes to their respective criminal codes to more successfully prosecute all those who sexually exploit children, both within their borders and beyond. Now, under Canadian and Italian law, there are strict criminal repercussions for Canadian and Italian nationals who travel overseas to exploit children for sexual purposes. This example proves that young people, if given the chance, can be a powerful force for change.

  The relevant changes to Canadian law can be found on the Department of Justice website: http://laws.justice.gc.ca/en/1997/16/5277.html – Chapter 16 (Bill 27) An Act to Amend the Criminal Code (Child Prostitution, Child Sex Tourism, Child Harassment and Female Genital Mutilation).

- Write letters to the tourism industry pressuring it to adopt self-regulatory measures and professional codes of conduct.
- Conduct research, raise awareness and educate your family, friends and neighbours.
- Join campaigns by non-governmental organisations and child rights campaigners, such as ECPAT, who are advocating for changes in laws and policies and working to assist child victims with recovery and reintegration into society.

- The above information is from Free the Children's website: www.freethechildren.com

Street children

Information from the Consortium for Street Children

Each child is unique

'They think every child who lives or makes a living in the streets is a bad child' 'I wish that our community and government would love us and guide us and not be ashamed of us'

(street children in the Philippines)

Who are 'street children'?

The term 'street children' is hotly debated. Some say it is negative – that it labels and stigmatises children. Others say it gives them an identity and a sense of belonging. It can include a very wide range of children who: are homeless; work on the streets but sleep at home; either do or do not have family contact; work in open-air markets; live on the streets with their families; live in day or night shelters; spend a lot of time in institutions (e.g. prison). The term 'street children' is used because it is short and widely understood. However, we must acknowledge the problems and wherever possible we should ask the children what they think themselves. In reality, street children defy such convenient generalisations because each child is unique.

How many are there?

Nobody knows. Street children are not easy to count because: they move around a lot, within and between cities; they are often excluded from 'statistic-friendly' infrastructures (schools, households etc.); definitions of 'street children' are vague and differing. Numbers of 'street children' have often been deliberately exaggerated and mis-

---

Street children are not easy to count because: they move around a lot, within and between cities; they are often excluded from 'statistic-friendly' infrastructures

---

quoted in order to sensationalise and victimise these children. Street children have the right to be accurately represented. City-level surveys conducted by local organisations and supported by a clear definition are more reliable. In many countries, there is anecdotal evidence that numbers are increasing, due to uncontrolled urbanisation (linked to poverty), conflict and children being orphaned by AIDS. Most statistics are just estimates e.g. Kenya: 250,000; Ethiopia: 150,000; Zimbabwe: 12,000; Bangladesh: 445,226; Nepal: 30,000; India: 11 million (these are based on broad definitions of 'street children'). Regardless of the statistics, even one child on the streets is too many if their rights are being violated.

What about girls?

'I have been a street girl since my father made a "woman" of me. I carry on in the world but I am really dead'

(17-year-old girl)

In general there are fewer girls than boys actually living on the streets (studies indicate between 3% and 30% depending on the country). This is for several reasons. In many cultures, there is much greater pressure for girls to stay at home than boys. Research shows that girls will put up with abuse at home for longer than boys but that once girls make the decision to leave home, the rupture is more permanent than for boys. Girls are also less visible on the streets as they are often forced or lured into brothels. Even though there are fewer street-living girls than boys, they are extremely vulnerable to human rights abuses both on the street and when they are arrested. However, it is important to note that street boys are also at risk of sexual abuse and exploitation as well as girls.

Where are their families?

Relatively few street children are actually orphans (although these numbers are increasing in some countries due to AIDS). The majority of street children are still in contact with their families and/or extended families. Many of them work on the streets in order to contribute to their family's income. Those who run away often do so because of physical, psychological and/or sexual violence or abuse at home. Family breakdown is also common in the case of re-marriage and problems with step-parents. Importantly, many projects try to reunify street children with their families. However, this is a complex and frustrating task that requires much specialised counselling to address the root causes why the child ran away in the first place. Unfortunately, in many cases, reunification with the family fails, or is not in the best interests of the child. In these cases alternatives such as fostering, group homes and residential centres are needed. Street children are rarely alone, even if they

Street children are often at greatest risk of violence from those that are responsible to protect them

have no family contact: 'Here we do not have any kind of blood relation with each other. But when we are in the street with other friends, though we do not have any name for our relation, we are like a family. We are all actually members of our street family.' (Street Diary, Save the Children Fund UK Nepal, 2001)

What about the authorities?

Ironically, street children are often at greatest risk of violence from those that are responsible to protect them – the police and other authorities. Police often beat, harass, sexually assault and even torture street children. They may beat children for their money or demand payment for protection, to avoid false charges, or for release from custody. They may seek out girls to demand sex. For many street children, assaults and thefts by the police are a routine part of their lives. Some are even killed by police. Very rarely are those responsible brought to justice.

Victims, villains or heroes?

Many images and stories portray street children either as helpless victims, dangerous criminals or heroic survivors. The reality is usually somewhere in between. They show incredible resiliency and initiative in the face of desperate circumstances. They have to be resourceful and strong in order to survive. But some do not survive. Others can only do so by breaking the law. We should respect their individual stories and characteristics. Each child is unique.

Street children and the Convention on the Rights of the Child (CRC)

■ Probably no environment contributes more to potential violations of the CRC than a childhood and youth spent outside the institutional framework of family and school in the usually hostile environment of the streets.

■ The majority of articles in the CRC apply to street children because of their extreme poverty and particular vulnerability to the following: violence (Art. 19), disease (Art. 24), discrimination (Art. 2), sexual abuse and exploitation (Art. 34, 32), substance abuse (Art. 33), emotional deprivation (Art. 19, 31), exploitative and harmful child labour (Art. 32), denial of rights within the juvenile justice system (Art. 37, 40), arbitrary execution (Art. 6), torture (Art. 37), lack of access to education (Art. 28, 29) and healthcare (Art. 24) and lack of identity documents (Art. 7).

■ The CRC sets out a framework for protection that emphasises the family and community as having the main responsibility for caring for children (Art. 5, 18). The role of the state is to support and enable families and communities to fulfil this role. However, it is an unfortunate fact that in many cases families and communities are not protective and nurturing. In these cases, as for children living on the streets, the state then takes on a greater responsibility to fill the gap (Art. 20: 'A child temporarily or permanently deprived of his or her family environment...shall be entitled to special protection and assistance provided by the State').

■ In reality, it is often civil society organisations rather than governments that take on the burden of caring for these children. Increased cooperation and collaboration is required amongst Civil Society Organisations (CSO) in order to exchange lessons learned and good practices. It is also needed between CSOs and the state to ensure the sustainability of programmes and to address underlying socio-economic and discriminatory policies that perpetuate the street children phenomenon.

■ The above information is from the Consortium for Street Children's website: www.streetchildren.org.uk
© *Consortium for Street Children 2005*

Sexual exploitation

I'm a teenager – What happened to my rights?

By Stuart Halford, Anthea Lawson, Nicola Sharp and Simon Heap

There are three main inter-related forms of commercial sexual exploitation of teenagers. These are: prostitution, pornography, and trafficking for sexual purposes. According to the United Nations, child prostitution can be defined as: 'the act of engaging or offering the services of a child to perform sexual acts for money or other consideration with that person or any other person'.[1] Child pornography consists of material representation of children engaged in sexual acts, real or simulated, intended for the sexual gratification of the user. Sex trafficking is defined as: '. . . a pernicious form of slavery; it is the purchase of a body for sexual gratification and/or financial gain'.[2]

Children of all ages have been found to be subjected to sexual exploitation. But the teenage years are a particularly vulnerable time because it is often easy for those exploiting them to lie about their age and claim that they are over 18. Moreover, it is relatively easy to get access to adolescents, when they are not being accompanied by an adult, and lure them into an exploitative situation. And parents often consent to their teenage children being taken by traffickers. This is either because they are duped into believing their son or daughter is being recruited for a respectable job or because they are so poor or in debt that they think they have no choice but to consent to anything that will help increase the family income.

It is difficult to know how many children are being exploited, as the shame, stigma, fear of reprisal and lack of belief in the authorities means that many do not report it. But estimates suggest that globally up to two million children suffer sexual exploitation every year, the majority of them girls.[3] The lack of accurate figures means it is of course hard to know whether the incidence of sexual exploitation of children is increasing or not. But various factors have certainly made teenage children more vulnerable: the erroneous belief that HIV/AIDS can be cured by having sex with a virgin; sex tourism which targets children; the growing use of the internet for child pornography; the increasingly international and organised nature of criminal networks; and the use of sexual violence as a weapon of war. It is the children who are already marginalised – the poor, and the uneducated – who are most vulnerable to sexual exploitation because they and their families are the most desperate. Evidence suggests that, due to poverty, adolescents made decisions to work in the sex industry because they wanted to contribute to the family income and support sick or ageing relatives.

The effects of commercial sexual exploitation on teenagers include unwanted pregnancies, severe physical and psychological trauma including death, HIV/AIDS and other sexually transmitted diseases, and permanent psychological scars.[4] Children are beaten, kicked and raped by those who exploit them. They are more vulnerable to sexually transmitted diseases than adults, including HIV/AIDS. They are not in a position to demand safe sex and may not be educated about it either.

The campaigning organisation ECPAT[5] reports that the rate of HIV

infection among prostituted Nigerian girls deported from Italy in 2003 was in excess of 50 per cent. According to one Cambodian non-governmental organisation, as many as 70 per cent of the girls rescued from brothels have been infected with HIV.[6]

Plan's response

Plan, in association with ECPAT, is trying to tackle sexual exploitation. They have set up a project which, once it is up and running, will promote legal reform and improved law enforcement, raise awareness of commercial sexual exploitation of children, and build the capacity of local organisations to rehabilitate and reintegrate child victims.[7] exploitation

The psychological effects include guilt, shame, low self-esteem, mistrust, stigma, nightmares and depression. Some turn to drink and drugs; some attempt suicide.

Prostitution and pornography violate the child's right to be protected from sexual exploitation and abuse. In the Mekong region of South East Asia, it is thought that about a third of all sex workers are aged between 12 and 17.[8] In Mexico, more than 16,000 children are working as prostitutes, with the highest numbers in tourist areas. In Lithuania, 20-50 per cent of prostitutes are believed to be minors, with some as young as 11.[9] Thirty per cent of those trafficked from Moldova are teenage girls trafficked for commercial sexual exploitation.[10]

Demand for child sex workers can also increase when military personnel, peacekeeping forces and humanitarian staff are present. Vulnerable refugee children may be left with little other option than sex with military personnel or peacekeepers as a means of survival. For example, in 1992 in Mozambique, UN soldiers recruited girls as young as 12 into prostitution.[11] More recently the presence of NATO-led troops in Kosovo has caused an increase in the numbers of bars and nightclubs where girls as young as 16 are reportedly held captive and forced to sell sex to troops and business-men.[11] A study by the UN on the sexual exploitation of children during armed conflict found that the arrival of peacekeeping troops was associated with a rapid rise in child prostitution in half of the countries studied.[11]

The growth of internet use has fuelled the exploitation of children for pornography. In July 2004, 70 children were rescued from a porno-graphy syndicate in Laguna in the Philippines. The following month UNICEF reported that child porno-graphy in the Philippines was far more widespread than previously thought, and this is because of poverty, public acceptance of pornography and prostitution, lack of stringent laws, and technological advances which make pornography easier to produce and propagate.[12]

Although the majority of victims of child sexual exploitation are female, boys also suffer. Abuse and exploitation of boys are even less reported than that of girls. In Sri Lanka, and according to statistics from UNICEF and the International Labour Organisation, there are between 5,000 and 30,000 Sri Lankan boys who are used by Western paedophile sex tourists.[13] In the Dominican Republic and Haiti, boys reportedly stay with adult male tourists on the beaches. Taboos about homosexuality mean that boys may not be able to admit even to themselves that they have been abused.[14]

Estimates put the number of children being trafficked for use as cheap labour and prostitution at 1.2 million a year.[15] Girls as young as 13 are trafficked from Asia and Eastern Europe as 'mail-order brides'. Girls used as domestic workers are in danger of sexual abuse in the homes of their 'employers'. In Fiji, for example, UNICEF found that eight out of ten domestic workers reported sexual abuse by their employers.[16] The UN lists Mexico as the number one centre for the supply of young children to North America. The majority of these children are sent to international paedophile organisa-

tions and most over the age of 12 end up becoming prostitutes.[17]

Porous borders and improved communications help the traffickers with their grim and lucrative work. For example, immigration controls at the Paraguay-Brazil border are very difficult to patrol, and children are reportedly trafficked in both directions across it. Officials do not always request identification papers from unaccompanied children or from adults travelling with young children. Girls are reportedly trafficked from Thailand to South Africa via Singapore, while children from several African nations are trafficked to South East Asia via South Africa.[18] In Greece, studies have indicated that more than 40 per cent of the children working as prostitutes are from neighbouring or regional countries such as Uzbekistan, Kazakhstan, Armenia, Albania and Iraq.[19]

Children who are 'rescued' from sexual exploitation abroad continue to suffer. They can be treated as criminals who are in breach of laws against prostitution and illegal immigration, and can be imprisoned before being sent to their country of origin. Once back in their country of origin, they may be punished again, this time according to the laws and policies of their own countries for emigrating illegally.

Plan's response

Roslyn's story
Roslyn, aged 16, had been promised work as a model in Japan. She was being recruited in the Philippines with nine other underage 'models' when they were stopped at Port Matnog by security guards who suspected they were minors being trafficked. Roslyn was then taken to a halfway house supported by Plan in Port Matnog. She was provided with food, shelter and counselling there before going back to her family. She said that she had had no idea what being a model entailed, and knew only that the cost of her travel to Japan would be deducted from her wages when she started work.[20] 'Matnog is considered to be a strategic location for traffickers attempting to move their human cargo across land routes,' explains Cathy Seco from

Plan. 'Some 5,000 people disembark at the port every day, providing useful cover for the illegitimate trade. The halfway house here represents another line of defence against the people and organisations who exploit the very young and underage for profit.'

Manmaya's story
Manmaya, from Nepal, was married in 1994 at the age of 15. When her family had not heard from her or her husband for several years, her community attempted to find her. They learned she had been taken to a brothel in India and that her husband was in prison in Kathmandu. But the police could not help, because there were no documents proving Manmaya's existence. She had not received a marriage certificate because she was underage when she married, and for the same reason did not qualify for a citizenship certificate or passport. Registration of births had only been introduced after she was born.[21]

Phina's story
Phina, 13, from Uganda, was sexually abused. Her father Mukasa could not prove she was underage because she had not been registered at birth, so there was no case. 'If only I had registered my daughter at birth, I would have won the case. I would have protected her,' said Mukasa.[22] In many countries, sex with a girl under 16, whether she gives consent or not, is regarded as rape. But without a birth certificate to show she is underage, it is very hard to get a conviction.

One of the most important steps in the fight against sexual exploita-tion is ensuring that every child is registered, as Manmaya and Phina's stories UNICEF illustrate. Plan and UNICEF have undertaken a number of birth registration campaigns in countries where many children lack birth certificates to prove their age. If children are not officially registered, they are not only without proper protection from exploitation, but may grow up without access to civil rights and a formal education. In Senegal, Plan is working with a local organisation to get 5,000 street children enrolled. In Togo, Plan's work in 26 communities means that 14,000 children now have a birth certificate.[23]

The UN Convention on the Rights of the Child

Article 34 of the UN Convention on the Rights of the Child says that states must prevent children being coerced into unlawful sexual activity and the exploitative use of children in prostitution or pornography or other unlawful sexual practices. Article 35 says states must prevent the abduction, sale or trafficking of children.

An Optional Protocol specifically addressing the commercial sexual exploitation of children was adopted in 2000 and came into force in 2002.[24] For it to be effective, governments will have to act at national level. Governments need to enact and enforce laws that punish those who traffic and sexually exploit children, and they need to give humanitarian visas or grant refugee status to trafficked children. They need to cooperate internationally to prevent trafficking and deal with trafficked children more humanely.

References

1 World Health Organization, *Commercial Sexual Exploitation of Children: The Health and Psychosocial Dimensions* (written for the World Congress against Commercial Sexual Exploitation of Children, 1996), 10 cited by Youth Advocate Program International, Commercial Sexual Exploitation of Children (CSEC) and Child Trafficking, www.yapi.org/csec/

2 Women's Environment & Development Organization, *Root Causes: A Gender Approach to Child Sexual Exploitation* (written for the World Congress against Commercial Sexual Exploitation of Children, 1996) cited by Youth Advocate Program International, Commercial Sexual Exploitation of Children (CSEC) and Child Trafficking, www.yapi.org/csec/

3 Youth Advocate Program International, Commercial Sexual Exploitation of Children (CSEC) and Child Trafficking, www.yapi.org/csec/

4 See Asia: Joint Programme between ECPAT International and Plan on Commercial Sexual Exploitation of Children (CSEC) in Asia.

5 End Child Prostitution, Child Pornography and Trafficking of Children for Sexual Purposes (ECPAT).

6 ECPAT International www.ecpat.net/eng/CSEC/faq/faq.asp

7 See Asia: Joint Programme between ECPAT International and Plan on Commercial Sexual Exploitation of Children (CSEC) in Asia.

8 See: *Worst Forms of Child Labour Data*, Cambodia, www.globalmarch.org/worstformsreport/world/cambodia.html

9 Civil Dimension of Security, 53 CCDG 04 E, Original: English, NATO Parliamentary Assembly, Sub-Committee on Democratic Governance – The Fight Against Children Trafficking in Europe, Draft Report, Gudmundur Arni Stefansson (Iceland), Rapporteur, International Secretariat 5 May 2004 www.naa.be/Docdownload.asp?ID=128

10 The figures for child prostitution may be underestimates, given that research tends to focus on the more prominent areas where it is occurring – in brothels and on the streets and other public places. It is much more difficult to find out the extent to which children are being forced to work in flats, or from clubs or bars.

11 ECPAT UK, www.ecpat.org.uk/child prostitution.htm

12 UNICEF condemns child pornography www.unicef.org/philippines/news/statement pornography.html

13 Damitha Hemachandra, Many Children Still Abused and Neglected in Sri Lanka, *Daily Mirror*, 8 October 2003; quoted on www.childprotection.gov.lk/newsUpdate0810200301.htm and cited on (APCI.2.3) Commentary on Home Office CIPU Sri Lanka Country Report of October 2003, compiled by Christian Wolff, with expert guidance from Nicholas Van Hear.

14 UNICEF, *Profiting from abuse: an investigation into the sexual exploitation of our children*, 2001.

15 Free the Children, *Child Labour – The Situation* at www.freethechildren.org/youthinaction/child labour the situation.htm

16 Information from UNICEF: www.unicef.org/protection/index childlabour.html

17 See CATW Fact Book, citing Allan Hall, *The Scotsman*, 25 August 1998, as cited in Worst Forms of Child Labour Data, Mexico, www.globalmarch.org/worstformsreport/world/cambodia.html

18 ECPAT International www.ecpat.net/eng/CSEC/faq/faq.asp

19 ECPAT International, *A Step Forward*, 1999, quoted on www.globalmarch.org/worstformsreport/world/worst-form.html

20 Plan, *When the dream becomes a nightmare: child trafficking in the Philippines*.

21 Plan, Universal Birth Registration and Protection from Sexual Exploitation and Abuse.

22 Ibid.

23 *Plan News & Views*, May 2004, p6.

24 Protocol to the Convention on the Rights of the Child on the Sale of Children, Child Trafficking and Child Pornography http://www.unhchr.ch/html/menu2/6/crc/treaties/opsc.htm As of November 2003, 67 states had ratified it. Also, in 2000 the Protocol to Prevent, Suppress and Punish Trafficking in Persons, Especially Women and Children, was passed to supplement the United Nations Convention Against Transnational Organised Crime. Again, if this is to be effective it requires governments to act at the national level.

■ The above information is from *I'm a teenager – What happened to my rights?*, a publication from Plan UK. For further information, visit www.plan-international.org

Child sex tourism

Market research reveals how to inform travellers about child sex tourism

ECPAT UK's (End Child Prostitution, Pornography and Trafficking) recent research into travellers' understanding of child sex tourism has found that 54% had either seen child sex tourism on holiday or had read a lot about it, whilst 46% were aware of the issue, but had limited knowledge.

The Home Office-funded research was carried out with 38 people in four focus group discussions and aimed to discover their thoughts on campaigns run by organisations against child sex tourism. The research also aimed to find out if travellers would be put off from booking a holiday if the tour operator or travel agent told them that they were working to prevent child sex tourism.

Sixty-one per cent said they would not be deterred from booking the holiday, and 34% said that it would make them more likely to book the holiday. However, 5% said they would be less likely to book the holiday. Asked if they thought a tour operator should inform them about child sex tourism, and whether this information should relate to a specific destination, 75% said yes; 41% said they would like to know about the issue in general and 34% wanted destination specific information. But 9% said it would put them off going to a destination.

While the research aimed to understand travellers' views of child sex tourism, it also asked if they would report suspicious activities. Seventy-five per cent said they would report the incidence while they were still on holiday, 22% would report on their return home and 3% said they would not report at all. Twenty-three per cent said they would inform their tour operator (not all respondents were on holiday with a tour operator), 19% would tell the local police, 15% would inform the hotel manager or staff, 12% would tell local charities and 3% would ignore it. Furthermore, 89% said if they were given

The Sexual Offences Act 2003, which came into force on 1st May 2004, contains provision for the prosecution in the UK of Britons who offend against children overseas. This extra-territorial legislation repeals the original extra-territorial legislation contained in the Sex Offenders Act 1997. The Act also introduced a new order, the foreign travel order, which will enable the courts, in certain circumstances and on application from a chief officer of police, to prohibit those convicted of sexual offences against children aged under 16 from travelling overseas where there is evidence that they intend to cause serious sexual harm to children in a foreign country.

Travellers can report concerns to Crimestoppers in the UK. The number is free in the UK, but there may be charges from phones overseas. The number is 0800 555 111.

information about how to report the suspicion they would be more likely to report, while 11% said it would make no difference.

The results of this research will help ECPAT UK, and its partners, to provide appropriate and effective information to the travelling public on how they can help prevent and protect children from abuse when they are on holiday.

Notes:

1. ECPAT UK is a coalition of nine UK organisations: Anti-Slavery International, Barnardo's, Jubilee Campaign, NSPCC, The Body Shop Foundation, The Children's Society, Save the Children UK, UNICEF UK and World Vision UK.

2. The project was advised by a multi-agency advisory group consisting of: the Association of British Travel Agents (ABTA), Crimestoppers, the Federation of Tour Operators, Foreign and Commonwealth Office, Home Office, National Criminal Intelligence Service, Travel Weekly.

■ The above information is from ECPAT UK's website which can be found at www.ecpat.org.uk

© ECPAT UK (End Child Prostitution, Pornography and Trafficking)

Prevention through awareness

Campaigning on child sex tourism: a market research project. By Julia Valdambrini

Child sex tourism

Child sex tourism (CST) is the sexual exploitation of children by adults who travel from their own country to another usually less developed country and engage in sexual activities with the children there.[1] It is often referred to as the commercial sexual exploitation of children (CSEC) in tourism. CSEC includes prostitution, pornography and the trafficking and sale of children. CST is a form of child prostitution, an activity defined as the use of children for sexual gratification by adults for remuneration in cash or kind to the child, or a third party. Sometimes this is organised by an intermediary such as a boyfriend, pimp, family member, neighbour, employer or teacher and may not always involve an exchange of money. It can also include 'in kind' payments such as gifts, food or shelter. According to UNICEF,[2] an estimated one million children enter the commercial sex trade every year around the world.

The extent of the problem of CST is hard to quantify due to the illegal and often hidden nature of the crime. However, a survey carried

out by the World Tourism Organisation's Child Prostitution Watch recorded cases of CST from 68 countries, either as sending or receiving countries.[3] There are 64 ECPAT groups working on the issue worldwide which also indicates the extent to which CST is an issue. Extensive research by Julia O'Connell Davidson and Jackie Sanchez Taylor[4] also confirms that it is a very real problem on a global scale. They conducted fieldwork in the Costa Rica, Cuba, Dominican Republic, Goa, South Africa and Thailand involving interviews with child sex tourists, a number of whom were British. It is difficult to ascertain the actual numbers of British tourists involved as the nature of the crime means most go undetected. However, the British do account for a substantial percentage of international tourist arrivals worldwide[5] and their involvement cannot be underestimated.

Legal framework

The United Nations Convention on the Rights of the Child (UNCRC, 1989)[6] states that any person under the age of 18 is considered a child and should be protected against any form of sexual exploitation (Article 34). 192 countries, including the UK, have adopted the UNCRC and have agreed to take all appropriate national, bilateral and multilateral measures to protect children from all forms of sexual exploitation and sexual abuse. UN conventions are legally binding.

Differing, and lower, ages of consent are often cited as a defence for child sex abuse overseas. However, it is important to note that it is illegal to pay for the sexual services of a child in most countries of the world and in the UK, Costa Rica, the Gambia and Thailand the age stipulation is defined as under 18 years.[7]

In the UK it is illegal to engage in prostitution with a person under

the age of 18.[8] It is also illegal for UK citizens and residents to engage in sexual activity with children overseas, and extra territorial legislation[9] exists making it possible for a British citizen to be prosecuted in the UK for an offence committed abroad. Additionally, convicted child sex offenders are subject to certain requirements, one of which is having to notify the police whenever they intend to travel overseas for three days or more. The police can, and do, pass this informa-tion to other jurisdictions where there is a risk that the offender may offend whilst overseas. Recent legislation in the UK has also introduced a Foreign Travel Order which enables the courts to prohibit a child sex offender from travelling to particular countries or regions, in order to protect children overseas from serious sexual harm.

In practice there have been very few convictions to date in the UK[10] under extra-territorial legislation. This is due to a number of inhibiting factors such as the difficulty in gathering evidence, co-operation of local police forces, difficulty in locating witnesses, or the practicalities of bringing children to the UK to give evidence. Ideally, it is preferable if a person is brought to justice in the country where the offence took place and serves a sentence there. There is a greater impact on offenders if they know they can be arrested in the country and be subject to foreign legislation and sentencing. It also provides an effective warning to other potential offenders if they know police are vigilant. For the country itself, it shows a determination and willing-ness to prevent CST, not only to other countries and tourists, but also to those involved in the sex trade in that country, including the victims, instigators and perpetrators.

The collaboration on this research project of UK law enforce-ment stakeholders such as Crime-stoppers and NCIS, has been bene-ficial to researching further into the issue of intelligence gathering on travelling UK child sex offenders. Currently it is difficult to gain an accurate picture of the situation due to the transitory nature of the crime.

Convicted child sex offenders are subject to certain requirements, one of which is having to notify the police whenever they intend to travel overseas for three days or more

Offences may be committed whilst a person is on holiday for a short time and then returns home, hence making it difficult to make arrests. Added to which is the identified displacement phenomenon when countries re-nowned for this activity enact strong law enforcement measures, only for offenders to travel to other countries with weak legal provisions. It would therefore be beneficial for reports to be made in respect of UK travellers to a UK based agency in order to build up an accurate picture of this activity, in terms of locations and types of people involved. Part of the research has therefore been con-cerned with establishing whether UK tourists would be willing to a) report and b) use the Crimestoppers number. This would assist UK law enforcement in working together with overseas agencies.

The advantage for UK citizens, whether they are travellers or tour representatives working in destina-tion, of reporting to a UK-based hotline are numerous. This type of reporting process maintains the anonymity of the reportee and would be English-speaking, therefore reducing the apprehension ex-perienced if reporting to local police authorities. It takes less time and would avoid them having to get involved with the local legal process. The following section analysing the market research data indicates that this could indeed be a viable method that could be used in the process of crime prevention.

References
1 ECPAT UK definition.
2 UNICEF (2003) 'Faces of Explotia-tion'. End Child Exploitation Campaign.
3 Group Développement (2001) 'Child Sex Tourism Action Sur-vey'. ECPAT International.
5 ECPAT theme papers for the 1st World Congress (1996).
5 http://www.world-tourism.org/market_research/facts/barometer/january2004.pdf
6 http://www.unicef.org/crc/crc.htm
7 http://www.interpol.int/Public/Children/SexualAbuse/NationalLaws
8 Sexual Offences Act 2003, Part 1, Section 47.
9 Sexual Offences Act 2003, Schedule 2, Section 72.
10 Three.

■ The above information is an extract from *Prevention through awareness – Campaigning on child sex tourism: a market research project*, a pubication by ECPAT UK's website which can be found at www.ecpat.org.uk

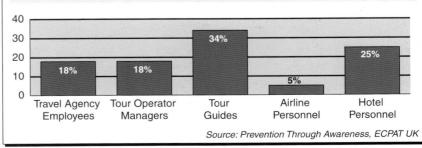

Responsibilities of the tourism industry

A Case Study on the Implementation of the Code of Conduct by the German Tour Operators – Tourists were interviewed about their awareness of commercial sexual exploitation of children

Who within the tourism industry should be especially qualified to inform tourists about commercial sexual exploitation of children?

Travel Agency Employees	18%
Tour Operator Managers	18%
Tour Guides	34%
Airline Personnel	5%
Hotel Personnel	25%

Source: Prevention Through Awareness, ECPAT UK

Global problem needs a global solution

John Carr reports on an international child protection conference

International child protection experts met in Bangkok November 2004 to discuss strategies to combat the rising problem of child prostitution and trafficking in East Asia and the Pacific. The conference, organised by Unicef, drew government representatives from China, Indonesia, Japan, South Korea, Australia, Vietnam, Cambodia, Philippines, Malaysia, Laos, Cambodia, Mongolia, the Solomon Islands, Papua New Guinea and Timor, and Thailand.

We were there to address a range of problems affecting children who get ensnared in commercial sexual exploitation across the region. In South East Asia armed criminal gangs simply walk across borders into countries such as Burma, Laos and Cambodia and kidnap children. These children are then trafficked to Bangkok and all points north, south, east and west, where they become sex slaves.

Some families sell some of their children to the gangs, condemning them to this kind of vile servitude. Other children either knowingly volunteer or are tricked into it, off the back of the promise of a well-paid job in a big city. Exactly which city, on which continent, does not always get mentioned.

This exploitation has been driven by white men from Europe and North America travelling to this region to rape children. But the newly affluent and increasingly mobile Chinese are also becoming a significant source of demand for the brothels that house young children based, among other things, on a belief that having sex with a virgin is a powerful charm against or a cure for HIV/Aids. This depressing scenario is exacerbated by poverty, and the comparative underdevelopment of government and police infrastructures for tackling child abuse across the region.

The criminal gangs trafficking children into Bangkok and elsewhere are also connected to the production of the child abuse images appearing on the internet and downloaded by paedophiles worldwide, including in Britain. The countries across the Far East and Pacific are keenly aware of how much their future prospects depend on their ability to use and have access to new technology, and therefore take the issue of online child abuse very seriously. The attitude and response of the Chinese government will be most crucial.

This exploitation has been driven by white men from Europe and North America travelling to this region to rape children

---

Figures from the UK's Internet Watch Foundation (IWF) clearly illustrate the global nature of internet paedophilia. The IWF monitors the origins of all illegal child abuse images reported in the UK. The USA and Russia predominate in this roll call of shame. Criminals in these countries are the biggest suppliers of child pornography on the planet. Only two other countries are sufficiently large producers to warrant a specific mention. One is Brazil, the other is South Korea, each at 4%, compared with 55% and 23% respectively for the USA and Russia.

The biggest ever police operation against online child pornography was against the Landslide website in Texas. A total of 250,000 men were found to have bought child pornography using their credit cards. They came from 59 different countries – and 7,200 names were from the UK. Three men were mainly responsible for supplying the images to Texas. One was Russian. The other two were Indonesian. Their names are known and were published. None of them was ever arrested.

The message from the conference was clear. We cannot parcel up child sexual exploitation – be it online or offline – into neat divisions. It raises a worldwide challenge and we need new and more effective laws and technology to act internationally.

■ John Carr is the internet adviser for the children's charity NCH

Global trends

Save the Children

The problem of child soldiers is most critical in Africa and Asia, though children are recruited and used as soldiers by government forces and armed groups in many countries in the Americas, Europe and the Middle East. However, a recent study by the ICRC, which included countries in all these regions, revealed that the over-whelming majority of a range of interviewees in countries affected by conflict believe that soldiers should be 18 years or older.

Despite a growing recognition of the problem, and substantial progress towards a commitment to protecting children in international law and other measures such as UN Security Council resolutions, evidence suggests that the number of child soldiers in the world is increasing.

This greater use of children in armed groups and forces is partially due to the current proliferation of prolonged conflicts. Children are more likely to be recruited as conflicts drag on and new recruits are needed. Communities become increasingly impoverished, and a 'culture of war' is often generated, where the distinction between combatants and civilians becomes blurred.

Children are also more at risk of joining armed groups and forces in wars taking place in developing countries and 'failed states'. First and foremost, poverty and related socio-economic factors are more prevalent in developing countries, where children are likely to have few livelihood options. Lack of access to education and the breakdown of society and traditional protective structures can also contribute to the recruitment of children, as can forced displacement and associated problems such as loss of livelihoods or educational opportunities. Children may also be motivated to join armed groups and forces for personal reasons of revenge, because of their own or others' expectations,

or to escape a violent home life. Conditions favouring the spread of HIV/AIDS often exist in communities ravaged by long-term warfare; the pandemic leaves many children without families and impoverished. Joining armies may be their only means of survival. However, in many cases children are abducted, forced or coerced to join, often in brutal circumstances.

Conflicts in developing countries often move quickly out of the international spotlight – so that parties involved in conflict are therefore under less scrutiny, and less pressure to respect international laws they may have signed and to fulfil their corresponding duties to protect citizens, including children. In these situations fewer resources are available to prevent and address violations of these laws, such as the recruitment of children into armed forces.

Key protection issues

The involvement of children in conflict exposes them to extreme and unacceptable threats to their health and well-being. With no one to protect them, children may be brutalised or killed by their commanders or peers. Boys and girls effectively lose their childhood and suffer terrible abuse, are exposed to hardship, desperate conditions and sexual violence. In combat, many children are killed, severely injured or permanently disabled. Some children may also be involved in committing human rights abuses, including war crimes and crimes against humanity. Children are deprived of growing up with their families and the opportunity to develop physically and emotionally in a familiar or protective, nurturing environment. They are denied their right to education. Child soldiers also risk long-term or even permanent separation from their families and communities, which makes them vulnerable to further violence, abuse and exploitation. Child soldiers not only suffer the direct impact of their experiences but also may be stigmatised or rejected by their communities, particularly if they have been involved in attacking them. Girls in particular often have enormous difficulties reintegrating into their families and communities, because of the kind of roles they may have been forced to play.

It is hard to imagine circumstances in which there is so much potential for abuse of children's rights. In summary, the involvement of children in armed forces represents or may lead to violations of the following fundamental rights of children as set down in the UNCRC:

- right to life, survival and development – Article 6
- right to preservation of identity – Article 8
- right to family unity – Article 9
- right to an opinion/ be consulted in all matters pertaining to the child – Article 12

- right to protection from physical or mental violence or exploitation – Article 19
- right to protection in case of separation from family – Article 20
- right to adequate standard of living for physical, mental, spiritual, moral and social development – Article 27
- right to education – Articles 28 and 29
- right to play – Article 31
- right to freedom from hazardous or exploitative labour – Article 32
- right to freedom from sexual exploitation or abuse – Article 34

- right to freedom from all other forms of exploitation prejudicial to welfare – Article 36
- right to freedom from torture or other cruel, inhuman or degrading treatment or punishment; and freedom from unlawful detention – Article 37
- right to protection under international humanitarian law in times of armed conflict, and right to freedom from military recruitment if under 15 – Article 38
- right to physical and psychological recovery and social reintegration of child victims of neglect, abuse or exploitation – Article 39

- right to fair judicial treatment taking into consideration the child's age and their reintegration into society – Article 40
- right to freedom from forced recruitment for all under-18s – Article 2, Optional Protocol.

■ The above information is an excerpt from *A Fighting Chance – Guidelines and implications for programmes involving children associated with armed groups and armed forces*, produced on behalf of the International Save the Children Alliance. Further copies of this report are downloadable from www.savethechildren.net

© Save the Children

War-affected children

Information from Free the Children

What is the problem?

In as many as 50 countries across the globe, children are caught up in armed conflicts – not only as bystanders, but as deliberate targets. These war-affected children are forced to kill or witness the killings of their own brothers, sisters, mothers, fathers, friends and neighbours, and are subjected to barbaric acts of physical, psychological and sexual cruelty. Their families, schools, neighbourhoods and communities are subjugated and destroyed, leaving them more vulnerable and forced to fend for themselves. One of the most alarming trends is the recruitment or abduction of children to serve as soldiers. Child soldiers serve as porters, spies, cooks, and messengers. Increasingly, however, children are forced to participate in combat, sometimes against family members or friends.

In the decade from 1986 to 1996, armed conflicts:
- Killed over 2 million children.
- Seriously injured or permanently disabled over 6 million.
- Orphaned over 1 million.
- Psychologically traumatised and scared over 10 million

In addition:
- Countless numbers of children,

especially girls, have been raped or subjected to other forms of sexual violence as a deliberate instrument of war.
- Currently, over 20 million children are displaced from their homes by wars. About 300,000 are exploited as child soldiers, and an estimated 800 are killed or maimed by landmines every month.

Why is this issue important?

- The involvement of children in armed conflict is a violation of the most basic ethical foundations of society.
- War violates every right a child should have – the right to life, the right to be with family and community, the right to health, the right to education, the right to the development of the

personality, and the right to be protected.
- Children and young people who are surrounded by violence are more likely to use violence to resolve issues. The violence, grief and anxiety suffered by children during armed conflict have negative effects on their mental health, quality of life and subsequent behaviour as adults.
- Children make up the majority of civilian victims of armed conflict, and the absolute numbers of children affected continue to grow.

Why are children increasingly becoming targets in armed conflicts?

- There is a higher proportion of civilian deaths in recent conflicts due to technology.
- Increasingly, conflicts are occurring within states as opposed to between states, and are often based on ethnicity. In ethnic conflicts, the distinction between combatant and non-combatant becomes blurred, and children and their families are likely to become deliberate targets.
- Many believe that children are easier to control, more obedient, easier to manipulate and less

likely to question orders than adults.

- Children are smaller than adults, and are less likely to be detected by the enemy.

What are the effects of armed conflict on children?

The effects of armed conflict on children depend to a large degree on three factors: age, gender, and context (i.e., the nature and extent of their involvement in armed conflict and their exposure to violence). The ways in which children may be affected include:

- Physical disability – resulting from mutilation, landmines, etc.
- Psychological trauna – war-affected children may suffer from a wide range of symptoms such as developmental delays, night-mares, lack of appetite and learning difficulties.
- Sexual abuse – girls and women are particularly vulnerable to sexual violence, including rape, sexual mutilation, forced prostitu-tion and forced pregnancy. As a result, there is increased risk of exposure to sexually transmitted diseases, including HIV/AIDS.
- Increased workloads, especially if a child has lost parents and other family members. In some cases, war-affected children may be heading households and taking care of their siblings. Child-headed households are particu-larly vulnerable to exploitative labour and prostitution.
- Increased threats to their survival from exposure to disease, mal-nutrition, and reduced access to or availability of basic health services.
- Loss of their homes, forcing them to flee, becoming either refugees or internally displaced persons. At least half of all refugees and internally displaced persons are children.

What is the relationship between globalisation and this issue?

Globalisation has helped to exacer-bate wars in many developing countries – wars that have in-creasingly involved children. There are at least three ways in which globalisation drives armed conflicts:

- The 'new economy of war' – the greater interconnectivity of the world and the increasing demand for goods and products have led to violent conflicts over natural resources such as diamonds (Sierra Leone and Angola) and oil (Sudan). None of these 'economies of war' would flourish without the demand or markets in more developed countries. Global businesses, some legal, some illegal, have helped to facilitate these wars, making them not just possible, but highly profitable.
- International weapons sales – the sale of weapons, especially small arms and light weapons (revolvers, rifles, grenades, anti-personnel landmines, etc.) has made it easier to wage wars. There are an estimated one-half billion small arms and light weapons that fuel armed conflicts around the world – 1 for every 12 people. The exact scale of the small arms and light weapons trade is not known. However, the legal trade is estimated to be worth about $6 billion, while the illegal trade is worth somewhere between $2 to $10 billion. Small arms are so accessible that even the poorest communities can acquire them and use children as soldiers. Weapons like the AK-47, for example, are so light and simple to operate that they make it very easy to turn children into soldiers.
- Debt and Structural Adjustment

Policies – the debt crisis in many developing countries and the package of policies to deal with this debt crisis (structural adjust-ment policies) have left many of these countries poorer and their citizens more discontented. This has helped to fuel military coups, unrest and sometimes armed conflict, which have increasingly involved children.

Testimonials – the voices of war-affected children:

'I was defiled by some older boys [could not remember how many] when we were being marched to the rebel camp. After returning from Sudan, I was the wife to one rebel commander, then another junior commander and then two "older" rebel soldiers. I had one child who died when he was a few days old. I was a slave to the rebels for 19 months. I do not think I will marry again.'

A (now 18-year-old) girl, abducted by the Lord's Resistance Army, a rebel group in Uganda.

'It is very difficult to live in war. You just wait for the moment you will die.'

Sanel, age 12, who lost an arm to a shell in Bosnia.

'They beat all the people there, old and young. They killed them all, nearly 10 people . . . like dogs they killed them . . . I didn't kill anyone, *but I saw them killing . . . the children who were with them killed too . . . with weapons . . . they made us drink the blood of people, we took blood from the dead into a bowl and they made us drink . . . then when they killed the people they made us eat their liver, their heart, which they took out and sliced and fried . . . And they made us little ones eat.'*

A Peruvian woman, recruited by the Shining Path (a guerrilla group) at age 11.

'I've seen people get their hands cut off, a 10-year-old girl raped and then die, and so many men and women burned alive. So many times I just cried inside my heart because I didn't dare cry out loud.'

A 14-year-old girl, abducted in January 1999 by the Revolutionary United Front, a rebel group in Sierra Leone.

What can you do to help your war-affected peers?

Advocacy:

■ Educate yourself – learn more about the issue of children and armed conflict. Conduct research, visit websites and gain a better understanding of the issue so that you can become an advocate for your war-affected peers.

Some useful resources include:
Youth Ambassadors for Peace website. See link on www.freethechildren.com
  State of the World's Children Report 1996. UNICEF.
  Impact of Armed Conflict on Children. Report of the Expert of the Secretary-General, Ms. Graca Mahel. (Report can be obtained from the following website: http://www.unicef.org/graca/).
  Website of the United Nations Secretary-General's Special Representative for Children and Armed Conflict (www.un.org/children/conflict).
  Coalition to Stop the Use of Child Soldiers (www.child-soldiers.org).
  Human Rights Watch (www.hrw.org).
■ Create greater awareness – with your newly acquired knowledge,

become a spokesperson and advocate for war-affected children. Be the voice of the countless numbers of children who have been victimised by war. Let them know that they are not alone in their struggle.

'I would like to give you a message . . . please do your best to tell the world what is happening to us, the children, so that our children don't have to pass through this violence.'

15-year-old girl who escaped from the Lord's Resistance Army, a rebel group in Uganda.

You can become a spokesperson or advocate for war-affected children by, for example:
■ Setting up seminars and displays.
■ Giving speeches to school groups and community organisations.
■ Writing a song or poem.
■ Organising a march.
■ Writing a newspaper article.
■ Organising petitions, for example:
  – Urging governments to support the International Code of Conduct on Arms Transfers, which aims to control the production and flow of small arms and light weapons to conflict zones, particularly where there is evidence of gross violations of children's rights.
  – Urging governments to place greater emphasis on promoting a culture of peace, through peace education programmes and by challenging the popular enter-

tainment culture that glorifies violence and gun use. The best way to protect children from wars is to prevent them from happening in the first place.
  – Urging governments to sign up to and ratify the Optional Protocol to the Convention on the Rights of the Child on the Involvement of Children in Armed Conflict www.unicef.org/crc/annex1.htm). This optional protocol, which came into force in February 2002, raises the minimum age from 15 to 18 for direct participation in hostilities, for compulsory recruitment, and for any recruitment or use in hostilities by non-governmental armed groups.

Fundraising:

■ Help to raise funds to build schools in post-conflict zones. In many war-torn countries, the educational system has been destroyed. In Sierra Leone, for example, 70% of primary school students cannot attend school because their schools have been damaged or destroyed by conflict. Education is very important for the psychological recovery of war-affected children, as it restores a semblance of 'normalcy' to their lives. You can help to give a child affected by war a chance for a brighter future.
■ Help to raise funds to buy fitted limbs (prosthesis) or wheelchairs for children who have been disabled by armed conflict.
■ Work to collect school and health kits for war-affected children. Even when schools are available, many children are unable to attend because they cannot afford basic school or health items. Many students across Canada work to collect kits to help their war-affected peers to go to school.

'War is Not a Game' Campaign:
Participate in Free the Children's 'War is Not a Game' Campaign, which was launched last autumn.

■ The above information is from Free the Children's website: www.freethechildren.com
© 2003 Free the Children

Broken lives of the twilight children

By David Blair, in Gulu

As she prepared her bed for the night, the little girl's wide, frightened eyes shone through the darkness. Simple Aber, 12, huddled in a ragged strip of cloth, lying inches from a fetid heap of rubbish. 'My mother told me, "You must leave the village and sleep in the town because of the war. If you stay, you will be taken",' she said.

Simple is among 20,000 children, some as young as six, who stream into the town of Gulu in Uganda every night. This twilight procession of tiny, barefoot figures lives in fear of abduction.

For northern Uganda is the hunting ground of the Lord's Resistance Army (LRA), Africa's most brutal rebel group led by a self-styled prophet called Joseph Kony.

Since the onset of his campaign 18 years ago, the LRA has kidnapped 20,000 children, brainwashing and enslaving them for use as soldiers and sexual playthings. More than 10,000 have disappeared in the last two years.

Kony targets children, devoting his messianic energies towards the abduction, indoctrination and often murder of as many as possible.

The catastrophe inflicted is almost without parallel. At least 1.6 million people – virtually the entire rural population – have fled their villages for squalid refugee camps. The number of refugees has trebled since 2002 and exceeds the 1.2 million in Sudan's war-torn Darfur.

Simple sleeps on concrete outside Gulu district hospital – six miles from her village of Eriaga in the rebel-infested bush. Scores of children huddle around her.

They are trying to avoid the fate of Bosco Ayella, 15. The LRA kidnapped him when he was 12 and the terrified boy was dragged before a rebel commander. He told Bosco and four other captives that they were now LRA fighters.

'The rebels had five boys who were captured,' said Bosco. 'The commander ordered us to kill them. I said, "We can't kill them". The commander said, "If you won't kill them, we will kill you". The rebels picked up clubs and hoes. We asked for mercy and said we would kill those boys.'

Bosco and the other captives were handed clubs and ordered to 'crush their heads'.

> *Simple is among 20,000 children, some as young as six, who stream into the town of Gulu in Uganda every night. This twilight procession of tiny, barefoot figures lives in fear of abduction*

'We began hitting them. They were crying for mercy,' said Bosco. 'Their blood was going everywhere. They were crying out but no one was listening. We beat them to death. From that time on, I felt I could not eat meat. I started having nightmares.'

Bosco spent three years with the LRA. He soon fell under Kony's spell and even today the rebel's supposed supernatural powers exert a hold. 'Whenever Kony predicts something, it comes true. When he gives an order, if you fail to do it, you die immediately.'

But Bosco was determined to escape. The LRA operated from bases in neighbouring Sudan. Bosco managed to slip away and surrender to Sudanese soldiers. He was repatriated last month and is now at the Children of War Rehabilitation Centre in Gulu.

Here, 530 children who have escaped the LRA are given counselling and medical care before being reunited with their families.

Florence Lakot, 24, escaped last month with her daughter, Senasca, six. Her child was born in the bush, two years after Miss Lakot's abduction at the age of 16.

Like most of the LRA's female captives, she was given to a rebel commander as a 'wife' – his seventh. 'When I was first given to him, he said, "You despise me. You must be beaten". He got four tough boys to beat me with sticks until I was unconscious. He did this twice. He said this was to beat the civilian out of me and make me a soldier,' said Miss Lakot.

After eight years with the LRA, she managed to surrender alongside some rebel commanders. All LRA fighters, including Kony, are eligible for an amnesty if they turn themselves in.

The rebellion grew from the grievances of the Acholi people, who believed that President Yoweri Museveni's government was discriminating against them.

Kony merged this resentment with religious fanaticism. But he never offered coherent demands, pledging only to rule according to the Ten Commandments. Today, his rebellion has no aim except rebellion itself. No one in Gulu doubts that if Kony surrendered, the war would end.

The clinic inside Gulu's rehabilitation centre displays dozens of photographs of children mutilated by rebels – infants without noses, lips, hands or feet.

Tabitha Ochen, the nurse, has treated many of them. Asked whether she could forgive Kony, she replied: 'Yes, I have already forgiven him.'

Stop the use of child soldiers!

Information from Human Rights Watch

In dozens of countries around the world, children have become direct participants in war. Denied a childhood and often subjected to horrific violence, some 300,000 children are serving as soldiers in current armed conflicts. These young combatants participate in all aspects of contemporary warfare. They wield AK-47s and M-16s on the front lines of combat, serve as human mine detectors, participate in suicide missions, carry supplies, and act as spies, messengers or lookouts.

Physically vulnerable and easily intimidated, children typically make obedient soldiers. Many are abducted or recruited by force, and often compelled to follow orders under threat of death. Others join armed groups out of desperation. As society breaks down during conflict, leaving children no access to school, driving them from their homes, or separating them from family members, many children perceive armed groups as their best chance for survival. Others seek escape from poverty or join military forces to avenge family members who have been killed.

Child soldiers are being used in more than thirty countries around the world. Human Rights Watch has interviewed child soldiers from countries including Angola, Colombia, Lebanon, Liberia, Sierra Leone, Sudan and Uganda. In Sierra Leone, thousands of children abducted by rebel forces witnessed and participated in horrible atrocities against civilians, including beheadings, amputations, rape, and burning people alive. Children forced to take part in atrocities were often given drugs to overcome their fear or reluctance to fight.

In Colombia, tens of thousands of children have been used as soldiers by all sides to the country's ongoing bloody conflict. Government-backed paramilitaries recruit children as young as eight, while guerrilla forces use children to collect intelligence, make and deploy mines, and serve as advance troops in ambush attacks.

Denied a childhood and often subjected to horrific violence, some 300,000 children are serving as soldiers in current armed conflicts

---

In southern Lebanon, boys as young as twelve years of age have been subject to forced conscription by the South Lebanon Army (SLA), an Israeli auxiliary militia. When men and boys refuse to serve, flee the region to avoid conscription, or desert the SLA forces, their entire families may be expelled from the occupied zone.

Girls are also used as soldiers in many parts of the world. In addition to combat duties, girls are subject to sexual abuse and may be taken as 'wives' by rebel leaders in Angola, Sierra Leone and Uganda. In Northern Uganda, Human Rights Watch interviewed girls who had been impregnated by rebel commanders, and then forced to strap their babies on their backs and take up arms against Ugandan security forces.

Because of their immaturity and lack of experience, child soldiers suffer higher casualties than their adult counterparts. Even after the conflict is over, they may be left physically disabled or psychologically traumatised. Frequently denied an education or the opportunity to learn civilian job skills, many find it difficult to re-join peaceful society. Schooled only in war, former child soldiers are often drawn into crime or become easy prey for future recruitment.

■ The above information is from Human Rights Watch's website which can be found at www.hrw.org

Voices of young soldiers

Information from Coalition to stop the use of Child Soldiers

Africa

Democratic Republic of the Congo

'Being new, I couldn't perform the very difficult exercises properly and so I was beaten every morning. Two of my friends in the camp died because of the beatings. The soldiers buried them in the latrines. I am still thinking of them.'

Former child soldier interviewed in 2002.

Sudan

'I joined the SPLA when I was 13. I am from Bahr Al Ghazal. They demobilised me in 2001 and took me to Rumbek, but I was given no demobilization documents. Now, I am stuck here because my family was killed in a government attack and because the SPLA would re-recruit me. At times I wonder why I am not going back to SPLA, half of my friends have and they seem to be better off than me.'

Boy interviewed by Coalition staff, southern Sudan, February 2004.

Uganda

'Early on when my brothers and I were captured, the LRA [Lord's Resistance Army] explained to us that all five brothers couldn't serve in the LRA because we would not perform well. So they tied up my two younger brothers and invited us to watch. Then they beat them with sticks until two of them died. They told us it would give us strength to fight. My youngest brother was nine years old.'

Former child soldier, aged 13.

Zimbabwe

'There was no one in charge of the dormitories and on a nightly basis we were raped. The men and youths would come into our dormitory in the dark, and they would just rape us – you would just have a man on top of you, and you could not even see who it was. If we cried afterwards, we were beaten with hosepipes. We were so scared that we did not report the rapes The youngest girl in our group was aged 11 and she was raped repeatedly in the base.'

19-year-old girl describing her experience in the National Youth Service Training Programme.

Asia/Pacific

India

'He had to run away to a forest with his friend to join the underground. He was 14 when he first held a gun in his hands. He said he loves to go to school but for the poverty of his family he has to lift a gun. Now he is earning enough money with the help of the gun for himself and to send money for his family also.'

Report of interview with 16-year-old boy, north-east India, 2004.

Indonesia, Nanggroe Aceh Darussalam province (Aceh)

'I know the work [monitoring the apparatus] is dangerous, and my parents had tried to stop me from getting involved. But I want to do something for the nanggroe therefore I was called for the fight. I am ready for all risks.'

Boy interviewed in March 2004: worked as an informant for the armed political group Free Aceh Movement, to spy on the Indonesian military when he was 17 years old.

Myanmar (Burma)

' . . . other trainees, if they were caught trying to run away their hands and feet were beaten with a bamboo stick and then put in shackles and beaten and poked again and again and then they were taken to the lock-up.'

Boy abducted at age 13 by government forces, interviewed in 2003.

Sri Lanka

'I ran away (to join an armed group) to escape a marriage I didn't like.'

Girl soldier in Sri Lanka.

Europe

Chechen Republic of the Russian Federation

'Russia has turned us into cattle. It is driving our youth into the arms of whoever comes along first and says "Go with us".'

Mother in Chechnya.

Latin America

Colombia

'They give you a gun and you have to kill the best friend you have. They do it to see if they can trust you. If you don't kill him, your friend will be ordered to kill you. I had to do it because otherwise I would have been killed. That's why I got out. I couldn't stand it any longer.'

17-year-old boy, joined paramilitary group aged 7, when a street child.

'I joined the guerrilla to escape . . . I thought I'd get some money and could be independent.'

17-year-old girl soldier with the Revolutionary Armed Forces of Colombia, interviewed in 2002.

Middle East and North Africa

Iraq

'I joined the Mahdi army to fight the Americans. Last night I fired a rocket-propelled grenade against a tank.'

A 12-year-old boy in Najaf, 2004.

Israel/Occupied Palestinian Territories

'I was detained on 18 March 2003 . . . We are in a very small room with 11 people . . . We are allowed to use the bathroom only three times a day at specific times. Once a week we are allowed to take a 30-minute recess. The prison guards force us into shabeh position: they tie our hands up and one leg and then we have to face the wall.'

15-year-old boy arrested by Israeli forces, reporting on detention conditions in an Israeli settlement outside Ramallah, April 2003.

■ The above information is from Coalition to Stop the Use of Child Soldiers' website: www.child-soldiers.org

© Coalition to Stop the Use of Child Soldiers

Governments failing generations of children

New global report finds child soldiers in over 20 conflicts worldwide

Governments are undermining progress in ending the use of children as soldiers, said a coalition of the world's leading human rights and humanitarian organisations in a newly published report.

The Coalition to Stop the Use of Child Soldiers (17 November 2004) released the most compre-hensive global survey of child soldiers to date. It said that children are fighting in almost every major conflict, in both government and opposition forces. They are being injured, subjected to horrific abuse and killed.

The Coalition accused govern-ments at the European Union, G-8 and UN Security Council of a failure of leadership. It called for the immediate enforcement of a ban on the use of child soldiers.

'Children should be protected from warfare not used to wage it. Instead generations are having their childhoods stolen by governments and armed groups,' said Casey Kelso, head of the Coalition to Stop the Use of Child Soldiers.

'A world that does not allow children to fight wars is possible, but governments must show the political will and courage to make this happen by enforcing international laws.'

Child Soldiers Global Report 2004 reviews trends and develop-ments since 2001 in 196 countries. Despite some improvements the situation remained the same or deteriorated in many countries. Wars ending in Afghanistan, Angola and Sierra Leone led to the de-mobilisation of 40,000 children, but over 25,000 were drawn into conflicts in Côte d'Ivoire and Sudan alone.

Opportunities for progress, including the creation of and growing support for a UN child soldiers treaty, the creation of demobilisation programmes in some countries and momentum towards prosecutions of

Amnesty International

those recruiting children, have been undermined by governments actively breaking pledges or failing to show political leadership.

Although the UN Security Council has condemned child soldiering and monitors those using children in war, some members have blocked real progress by opposing concrete penalties for violators. The Coalition said that the Security Council should take immediate and decisive action to get children out of conflict by applying targeted sanc-tions and referring child recruiters to the International Criminal Court for prosecution.

Armed groups, both government-backed paramilitaries and opposition forces, are the main culprits in recruitment and use of child soldiers. Dozens of groups in at least 21 conflicts have recruited tens of thousands of children since 2001, forcing them into combat, training them to use explosives and weapons, and subjecting them to rape, violence and hard labour.

Girls and boys in the opposition Revolutionary Armed Forces of Colombia, for example, were subjected to 'war councils' for disciplinary offences and in some cases other children were forced to execute them. In eastern Democratic Republic of Congo, armed groups sexually abused and raped girls and forced children to kill their own relatives.

'Children should be protected from warfare not used to wage it'

The Coalition said that all armed groups should protect children from conflict or be held legally accountable.

Governments, including Burundi, Democratic Republic of Congo, Myanmar, Sudan and the USA, used children on the front lines in at least 10 conflicts. Others, including Colombia, Uganda and Zimbabwe, backed paramilitary groups and militias that used child soldiers. States such as Indonesia and Nepal used children as informants, spies or messengers.

Some governments, including Burundi, Indonesia and the Russian Federation, killed, tortured or arbitrarily detained children suspected of supporting armed opposition. Palestinian children detained by Israeli forces were tortured or threatened to coerce them to become informants.

Western governments broke commitments to protect children by providing military training and support to governments using child soldiers, such as Rwanda and Uganda.

The Coalition called on govern-ments to ban all recruitment of under-18s into any armed force and to ratify and fully implement the UN child soldiers treaty, which is helping to reduce the numbers of children used in hostilities.

At least 60 governments, including Australia, Austria, Germany, the Netherlands, the United Kingdom and the USA, continue to legally recruit children aged 16 and 17.

■ The above information is from an Amnesty International UK news release published on 17 November 2004. For more information visit their website which can be found at www.amnesty.org.uk

Children as weapons of war

Information from Human Rights Watch

By Jo Becker

Over the last five years, the global campaign to stop the use of child soldiers has garnered an impressive series of successes, including new international legal standards, action by the UN Security Council and regional bodies, and pledges from various armed groups and governments to end the use of child soldiers. Despite gains in awareness and better understanding of practical policies that can help reduce the use of children in war, the practice persists in at least twenty countries, and globally, the number of child soldiers – about 300,000 – is believed to have remained fairly constant.

As the end of wars in Sierra Leone, Angola, and elsewhere freed thousands of former child soldiers from active armed conflict, new conflicts in Liberia and Côte d'Ivoire drew in thousands of new child recruits, including former child soldiers from neighbouring countries. In some continuing armed conflicts, child recruitment increased alarmingly. In Northern Uganda, abduction rates reached record levels in late 2002 and 2003 as over 8,000 boys and girls were forced by the Lord's Resistance Army to become soldiers, labourers, and sexual slaves. In the neighbouring Democratic Republic of Congo (DRC), where all parties to the armed conflict recruit and use children, some as young as seven, the forced recruitment of children increased so dramatically in late 2002 and early 2003 that observers described the fighting forces as 'armies of children'.

In many conflicts, commanders see children as cheap, compliant, and effective fighters. They may be unlikely to stop recruiting child soldiers or demobilise their young fighters unless they perceive that the benefits of doing so outweigh the military advantage the children provide, or that the costs of continuing to use child soldiers are unacceptably high.

In theory, the benefits of ending child soldier use can include an enhanced reputation and legitimacy within the international community, and practical support for rehabilitation of former child soldiers, including educational and vocational opportunities. Possible negative consequences of continued child soldier use can include 'shaming' in international fora and the media, restrictions on military and other assistance, exclusion from governance structures or amnesty agreements, and prosecution by the International Criminal Court or other justice mechanisms.

In practice, however, the use of child soldiers all too often fails to elicit action by the international community at all, apart from general statements of condemnation. Human Rights Watch is aware of no examples of military aid being cut off or other sanctions imposed on a government or armed group for its use of child soldiers. Conversely, when armed forces or groups do improve their practices, benefits also frequently fail to materialise. Although governments and armed groups receive public attention for commitments to end use of child soldiers, concrete support for demobilisation and rehabilitation efforts often does not follow.

If the international community is serious about ending the use of child soldiers, it needs to build on the successes of the past five years, but with a sober eye for the obstacles that have stymied further progress. This essay gives an overview of developments over that period, both positive and negative, and offers suggestions on the way forward.

Renewed progress will depend on clearly and publicly identifying the responsible parties; providing financial and other assistance for demobilisation and rehabilitation; and, most importantly, ensuring that violators pay a price should they continue to recruit and deploy child soldiers.

■ The above information is from Human Rights Watch's website which can be found at www.hrw.org
© 2005 Human Rights Watch

- One out of six children in the world today is involved in child labour. (p. 1)

- Most people would agree that some types of child work are evidently wrong – working in coal mines, or rubbish tips, or glass factories. (p. 2)

- Trafficking involves transporting people away from the communities in which they live, by the threat or use of violence, deception, or coercion so they can be exploited as forced or enslaved workers for sex or labour. (p. 3)

- For many children, school is not an option. Education can be expensive and some parents feel that what their children will learn is irrelevant to the realities of their everyday lives and futures. (p. 4)

- In independent investigations in West Africa, Guatemala, El Salvador, and Malaysia/Indonesia, Human Rights Watch found that child domestics are exploited and abused on a routine basis. (p. 8)

- Domestic workers in Malaysia are not allowed outside of the house and many reported they were unable to write letters home, make phone calls, or practise their religion. (p. 9)

- Child domestics work under constant threat of punishment and physical abuse. (p. 10)

- Especially in developing countries, legal protection for child labourers does not extend beyond the formal sector to the kinds of work in which children are most involved, such as agriculture and domestic service. (p. 11)

- Education is the key to ending the exploitation of children. (p. 11)

- Research carried out in the hand-made carpet industry shows that the cost of replacing children with adults in factories only adds about 4% to the price of a carpet. (p. 12)

- All sexually exploited children suffer serious physical, psychological and social harm. (p. 16)

- 'The commercial sexual exploitation of children is a fundamental violation of children's rights. It comprises sexual abuse by the adult and remuneration in cash or in kind to the child or to a third person or persons. The child is treated as a sexual object and as a commercial object. The commercial sexual exploitation of children constitutes a form of coercion and violence against children, and amounts to forced labour and a contemporary form of slavery.' (p. 17)

- Street children are often at greatest risk of violence from those that are responsible to protect them – the police and other authorities. (p. 19)

- Estimates suggest that globally up to two million children suffer sexual exploitation every year, the majority of them girls. (p. 20)

- The effects of commercial sexual exploitation on teenagers include unwanted pregnancies, severe physical and psychological trauma including death, HIV/AIDS and other sexually transmitted diseases, and permanent psychological scars. (p. 20)

- States must prevent children being coerced into unlawful sexual activity and the exploitative use of children in prostitution or pornography. (p. 22)

- Africa has the largest number of child soldiers with up to 100,000 believed to be involved in hostilities in mid-2004. (p. 29)

- Research conducted in 1998 indicated that up to 300,000 children under the age of 18 were participating in armed conflict worldwide. (p. 29)

- This greater use of children in armed groups and forces is partially due to the current proliferation of prolonged conflicts. Children are more likely to be recruited as conflicts drag on and new recruits are needed. (p. 31)

- Currently, over 20 million children are displaced from their homes by wars. (p. 32)

- Globalisation has helped to exacerbate wars in many developing countries – wars that have increasingly involved children. (p. 33)

- Denied a childhood and often subjected to horrific violence, some 300,000 children are serving as soldiers in current armed conflicts. (p. 36)

- Because of their immaturity and lack of experience, child soldiers suffer higher casualties than their adult counterparts. Even after the conflict is over, they may be left physically disabled or psychologically traumatised. (p. 36)

- Children should be protected from warfare not used to wage it. Instead generations are having their childhoods stolen by governments and armed groups. (p. 38)

ADDITIONAL RESOURCES

You might like to contact the following organisations for further information. Due to the increasing cost of postage, many organisations cannot respond to enquiries unless they receive a stamped, addressed envelope.

Amnesty International – British Section
99 -119 Roseberry Avenue
London, EC1R 4RE
Tel: 020 7814 6200
Fax: 020 7 833 1510
E-mail: info@amnesty.org.uk
Website: www.amnesty.org.uk
A worldwide human rights movement which is independent of any government, political faction, ideology, economic interest or religious creed.

Anti-Slavery International
Thomas Clarkson House
The Stableyard
Broomgrove Road
London, SW9 9TL
Tel: 020 7501 8920
Fax: 020 7738 4110
E-mail: info@antislavery.org
Website: www.antislavery.org
The world's oldest international human rights organisation, founded in 1839.

ChildHope
Development House
56-64 Leonard Street
London, EC2A 4JX
Tel: 020 7833 0868
Fax: 020 7533 2500
E-mail: chuk@gn.apc.org
Website: www.childhopeuk.org
An international non-government organisation (NGO) dedicated to improving the lives and defending the rights of street children world-wide.

Coalition to Stop the Use of Child Soldiers
2nd Floor, 2-12 Pentonville Road
London, N1 9HF
E-mail: info@child-soldiers.org
Website: www.child-soldiers.org
An international movement of organisations and individuals committed to ending the use of children as soldiers.

Consortium for Street Children
Unit 306, Bon Marche Centre
241-251 Ferndale Road
London, SW9 8BJ
Tel: 020 7274 0087
Fax: 020 7274 0372
E-mail: info@streetchildren.org.uk
Website: www.streetchildren.org.uk
Consists of 35 UK-based organisations dedicated to the welfare and rights of street living and working children.

ECPAT UK
Thomas Clarkson House
The Stableyard
Broomgrove Road
London, SW9 9TL
Tel: 020 7501 8927
Fax: 020 7738 4110
E-mail: ecpatuk@antislavery.org
Website: www.ecpat.org.uk
ECPAT UK is part of an international network of ECPAT groups in over 40 countries.

Free the Children
233 Carlton Street
Toronto, Ontario M5A 2 L2
Canada
Tel: + 1 416 925 5894
Fax: + 1 416 925 8242
E-mail: info@freethechildren.com
Website: www.freethechildren.com
A unique international youth organisation that empowers young people through representation, leadership and action.

Human Rights Watch
2nd Floor
2-12 Pentonville Road
London, N1 9HF
Tel: 020 7713 1995
Fax: 020 7713 1800
E-mail: hrwuk@hrw.org
Website: www.hrw.org
Human Rights Watch is dedicated to protecting the human rights of people around the world.

Institute of Economic Affairs (IEA)
2 Lord North Street
London, SW1P 3LB
Tel: 020 7799 3745
Fax: 020 7799 2137
E-mail: iea@iea.org.uk
Website: www.iea.org.uk
The IEA's goal is to explain free-market ideas to the public, including politicians, students, journalists, businessmen, academics and anyone interested in public policy.

International Labour Office (ILO)
Millbank Tower
21-24 Mill Bank
London, SW1P 4QP
Tel: 0207 828 6401
Fax: 0207 233 5925
E-mail: london@ilo.org
Website: www.ilo.org
The United Nations agency with global responsibility for work, employment and labour market issues.

Plan UK
2nd Floor, 5-6 Underhill Street
London, NW1 7HS
Tel: 020 7485 6612
Fax: 020 7485 2107
E-mail: mail@plan-international.org
Website: www.plan-uk.org
An international, humanitarian, child-focussed development organisation with no religious, political or governmental affiliations.

Save the Children
1 St John's Lane
London, EC1M 4AR
Tel: 020 7012 6400
Fax: 020 7012 6963
E-mail: enquiries@scfuk.org.uk
Website: www.savethechildren.org.uk
The leading UK charity working to create a better world for children.

United Kingdom Committee for UNICEF
Africa House
64-78 Kingsway
London, WC2B 6NB
Tel: 0207 405 5592
Fax: 0207 405 2332
E-mail: info@unicef.org.uk
Website: www.unicef.org.uk
UNICEF, the United Nations Children's Fund, is a global champion for children's rights.

INDEX

ACKNOWLEDGEMENTS

The publisher is grateful for permission to reproduce the following material.

While every care has been taken to trace and acknowledge copyright, the publisher tenders its apology for any accidental infringement or where copyright has proved untraceable. The publisher would be pleased to come to a suitable arrangement in any such case with the rightful owner.

Chapter One: Child Labour

Facts on child labour, © International Labour Organization, Faces of exploitation, © UNICEF UK, Child labour, © Anti-Slavery International, Child labour on sugar plantations, © Human Rights Watch, The ILO and the fight against child labour, © International Labour Organization, Children as domestic labourers, © International Labour Organization, Child domestics, © Human Rights Watch, Economically active children, © International Labour Organization/United Nations Population Division, Child labour – what can be done?, © 2005 Free the Children, Children engaged in child labour, © International Labour Organization, Child labour, © ChildHope, Economic truths of child labour, © Institute of Economic Affairs, Eliminating child labour, © International Labour Organization.

Chapter Two: Sexual Exploitation

Commercial sexual exploitation, © UNICEF, Sexual exploitation, © 2005 Free the Children, Street children,
© Consortium for Street Children 2005, Sexual exploitation, © Plan UK, Child sex tourism, © ECPAT UK, Prevention through awareness, © ECPAT UK, Responsibilities of the tourism industry, © ECPAT UK, Global problem needs a global solution, © Guardian Newspapers Limited 2004, Fighting sexual exploitation and trafficking, © UNICEF, Worst forms of child labour, © International Labour Organization.

Chapter Three: Child Soldiers

Child soldiers, © Coalition to Stop the Use of Child Soldiers, Child soldiers in armed conflict, © Coalition to Stop the Use of Child Soldiers, Global trends, © Save the Children, War-affected children, © 2005 Free the Children, Broken lives of the twilight children, © Telegraph Group Limited, London 2005, Stop the use of child soldiers!, © 2005 Human Rights Watch, Voices of young soldiers, © Coalition to Stop the Use of Child Soldiers, Governments failing generations of children, © Amnesty International UK, Children as weapons of war, © 2005 Human Rights Watch.

Photographs and illustrations:

Pages 1, 23, 31, 39: Simon Kneebone; pages 5, 26: Pumpkin House; pages 12, 33: Bev Aisbett; pages 14, 27, 36: Don Hatcher; pages 17, 24: Angelo Madrid.

Craig Donnellan
Cambridge
April, 2005